S0-BCA-380

Southern Front

Bilingual Press/Editorial Bilingüe

General Editor
    Gary D. Keller

Managing Editor
    Karen S. Van Hooft

Senior Editor
    Mary M. Keller

Assistant Editor
    Linda St. George Thurston

Editorial Board
    Juan Goytisolo
    Francisco Jiménez
    Eduardo Rivera
    Severo Sarduy
    Mario Vargas Llosa

Address:
Bilingual Review/Press
Hispanic Research Center
Arizona State University
Tempe, Arizona 85287
(602) 965-3867

Southern Front

Alejandro Murguía

Bilingual Press/Editorial Bilingüe
TEMPE, ARIZONA

© 1990 by Bilingual Press/Editorial Bilingüe

All rights reserved. No part of this publication may be reproduced in any manner without permission in writing, except in the case of brief quotations embodied in critical articles and reviews.

ISBN: 0-916950-97-2

Library of Congress Cataloging-in-Publication Data

Murguía, Alejandro, 1949-
    Southern front / Alejandro Murguía
        p.   cm.
    ISBN 0-916950-97-2
    1. Nicaragua—History—Revolution, 1979—Fiction.   I. Title.
PS3563.U7255S6   1989
813.54—dc20   89-7336
                                                                              CIP

PRINTED IN THE UNITED STATES OF AMERICA

Cover design by Peter J. Hanegraaf
Back cover photo by Michele Maria Boleyn

Acknowledgments

This volume is supported by a grant from the National Endowment for the Arts in Washington, D.C., a Federal agency.

The author and editors wish to acknowledge the first appearance of several of these stories in slightly different form in the following magazines:

"33," in *Oro Madre* (Fremont, CA), Vol. 1, No. 4 (Fall 1982);
"Squad Leader," in *Oro Madre*, Vol. 2, No. 1 (Summer 1983);
"In the South," in *Humanizarte* (Oakland, CA), Vol. 8, No. 2 (Summer 1987);
"In the South" (excerpt), in *City Lights Review* (San Francisco, CA), No. 1 (1987).

Contents

Author's Note

The following are some Central American regionalisms, colloquialisms, and military terms whose meanings may be unknown to the reader of this work and whose definitions will not be found in standard dictionaries:

BECAT, Batallón Especial Contra Ataques Terroristas. Somoza's main counterinsurgency unit.

chele, Nicaraguan slang for a light-skinned, blond-haired person; what Chicanos call a güero.

chilíncocos, seeds from tropical palms, similar to dates.

compa, compita, compañero.

Euskara, the Basque language.

garobo, a reptile similar to the iguana, but smaller and darker in color.

Jerry can, a 5- or 10-gallon military container used mostly for gasoline. Of World War II German origin, but popularized and named by the British, hence the name Jerry can.

Nica, slang for Nicaraguan.

oreja, literally, an "ear" for the dictatorship, i.e., an informer.

Pana, slang for Panamanian.

pinolero, from the drink pinol, the typical Nicaraguan drink made from ground toasted corn, sugar, water, and ice. Pinolero means to be very Nicaraguan.

P.L.O.M., Patria Libre o Morir, the slogan of the Sandinistas.

responsable, the person responsible for a specific action, task, or site.

rigola, a word from the Dominican Republic which means irrigation ditch or canal; also a slang word for the place in the fields where campesinos gather after work.

Tica or **Tico,** Central American slang for a native of Costa Rica.

Tico-Nica, a person of Costa Rican and Nicaraguan descent.

vigorón, typical Nicaraguan dish made with chicharrón, cooked yucca, and grated cabbage marinated in vinegar.

Wing Chun, According to legend, Wing Chun (beautiful spring-time) was founded by a Chinese nun, Yim Wing Chun, 400 years ago. It is a martial art based on dynamic tension techniques.

"Yhay," typical Nicaraguan greeting. A Chicano equivalent would be "queúbole" or "quiúbole" (= ¿Qué húbole?).

To the heroic Nicaraguan people
and their vanguard,
the Frente Sandinista de Liberación Nacional,
and to all the internationalists
on all the fronts of war.

Foreword

The Southern Front refers to the area along the Nicaraguan-Costa Rican border during the war against the Somoza family regime and its last patriarch, Anastasio Somoza Debayle, which culminated on July 19, 1979, with the victorious insurrection of the Nicaraguan people led by the Frente Sandinista de Liberación Nacional (FSLN). The combat zone stretched from the mouth of the San Juan River, which spills into the Caribbean at San Juan del Norte, to San Juan del Sur on the Pacific Ocean. It involved the ports of San Carlos and San Miguelito on Lake Nicaragua as well as the Archipelago of Solentiname. It included the villages, hamlets, border garrisons, and outposts of Los Chiles, El Castillo, Los Sábalos, Orosí, Cárdenas, El Naranjo, El Ostional, Peñas Blancas, Sapoá, Boca de Sapoá, La Calera, and Sotacaballo; the hills known as La Cimarrona, Colina 155, and Colina 50; and the towns of La Virgen and Rivas, the capital of the Department of Rivas. It was a fluid and constantly changing guerrilla front, and yet it had the distinction of being the only front where a traditional war of positions was fought. In its early years of formation, the Southern Front was organized as far north as Masaya, where its first comandante, Camilo Ortega Saavedra, along with the compañeros Moisés Rivera and Arnold Quant Ponce, were killed by the National Guard in Monimbó on February 26, 1978. The last comandante of the Southern Front was Edén Pastora, known as Comandante Cero, who later betrayed the Nicaraguan revolution.

If there was one single characteristic of this front that made it unique, it was the large participation of international volunteers. At one time or another, with varying degrees of success, there were Panamanian, Costa Rican, and Venezuelan brigades at the front. On a more individual level, there were Panamanian, Costa Rican,

Colombian, Chilean, Venezuelan, Salvadoran, Honduran, Cuban, Spanish, West German, Swiss, Swedish, Italian, Portuguese, and Mexican volunteers, among the nationalities known to this author. From the United States, Nicaraguan Americans, Cuban Americans, Puerto Ricans, and over a half dozen Chicanos participated in the Southern Front. There was also a contingent of Mexican doctors as well as an international group of photojournalists and filmmakers who left a visual record of the war in the south. A significant number of the international volunteers were women.

The first major combat in the Southern Front occurred in the early morning hours of October 17, 1977, when the FSLN attacked and destroyed the National Guard barracks at San Carlos. The dictatorship responded by burning and destroying the contemplative commune that had been founded on the Archipelago of Solentiname by the poet-priest Ernesto Cardenal.

In February 1978, the Southern Front forces took and briefly held the city of Rivas. As the war intensified against the dictatorship, it became necessary for the insurgents to hold a piece of Nicaraguan territory so as to declare a provisional government. The efforts to establish a liberated zone became focused on the border town of Peñas Blancas.

Peñas Blancas was the most important border crossing along Nicaragua's southern frontier; it was the main port of entry and departure, sitting right on the Pan American Highway. Whoever controlled Peñas Blancas controlled access to Nicaragua from the south. At the peak of the insurrection of 1978, on September 17th, the Southern Front wrested control of Peñas Blancas from the National Guard in a 9-hour pitched battle but was forced to withdraw when National Guard reinforcements were able to cross the Río Pita.

On May 23rd, 1979, the columns of the Southern Front opened the Final Offensive with the taking of the National Guard garrison at El Naranjo. After weeks of fighting in the hill country, the Front regrouped and took Peñas Blancas for the second time on June 12th. The following day it took Sapoá before halting on the banks of the Río Ostallo; in the interior, another column lay siege to Rivas for the remainder of the war. The total number of combatants at the Southern Front never numbered more than 800, and they held off some

2,000 National Guard troops, including 500 elite forces of the Escuela de Entrenamiento Básico de Infantería (EEBI), led by the infamous Comandante Bravo.

My first contact with the leaders of the Southern Front occurred in October 1978 on a return trip from an international conference of solidarity with the people of Nicaragua held in Panama City. It was through the contacts of Casimiro Sotelo, then a member of "Los Doce," that I initiated a series of projects with "Mauricio," who was channeling all the international aid arriving in San José, Costa Rica. It was during that stay, while at the house of Ernesto Castillo, that late one night, 2 haggard and weary comandantes made an appearance to give a press conference for foreign journalists. That night I taped one of the first interviews given for the international press by Daniel Ortega Saavedra and Víctor Tirado López, who had just come out of the Southern Front after the insurrection of September.

During the period between October 1978 and June 1979, I devoted full time to organizing solidarity committees across the United States in support of the Nicaraguan people, as well as editing the journal, *Gaceta Sandinista.* In June of 1979, along with the compañeros "Armando" and "Danilo," I left for Costa Rica to join in the Final Offensive.

When we first entered the Southern Front, our duties entailed the unloading of supply planes flying into small airstrips in Costa Rica and the guarding of munitions stocks in security houses. Later, inside Nicaragua, I helped train a platoon of riflemen, the majority of whom only days before had been your typical, average Central Americans, strolling along a plaza or making plans to meet friends in the evening. The men and women of the Southern Front were not soldiers by trade, but it was a profession they had to learn overnight. In early July 1979, the Somocistas launched their long-awaited counteroffensive aimed at dislodging the FSLN and its combatants from the border area. Due to the high casualty rate, there were not enough experienced combatants at the front, so I was placed in charge of a squad of mostly teenaged Nicaraguans and not much older internationalists attached to the General Staff of the Southern Front in Peñas Blancas. I am not boasting when I say that every member of my squad came out alive. It is merely a statement. Too many good people died in El Ostional, El Naranjo, Peñas Blancas, and Sapoá for the survivors to boast of their luck.

The stories in this collection take place during the time of the Final Offensive; they are set in the liberated zone that stretched from Peñas Blancas to Sapoá and included the Boca de Sapoá and the nearby village of Cárdenas, which was taken, lost, and retaken—an area approximately 6 km long by 3 km wide. Several stories were written in the days following the 19th of July, although due to time, distance, and circumstances, only "33," "Heavy Weather," and "Squad Leader" survive in any form.

So much happened on the Southern Front that obviously not everything could be mentioned in this small collection. I leave it to the other participants to tell those stories. Finally, it is important to point out that although these stories are based on true events, the action and characters are fictional.

These, then, are the stories of the Chicano internationalist who fought shoulder to shoulder with the Nicaraguans in the Southern Front Benjamín Zeledón.

A. M.

"In war you cover yourself with glory
Or you cover yourself with shit."

—Anonymous combatant of the Southern Front

In the South

A red sunset streaked the sky above the coffee-growing mountain peaks that circle San José, Costa Rica. The white Toyota jeep headed up the winding Pan American Highway as the last of the orange light broke through crimson clouds, and fireflies, like tracers, shot out of the darkened countryside. The windshield wipers flicked the last drops of rain away and stopped. Five were cramped in the cab of the jeep; 2 rode silently in front watching the underbrush pass by. Ulises leaned back against the jeep cab listening to the sibilant sound of the tires on the wet highway, cracked leather Gladstone bag resting between his feet, jean cuffs pulled over boot tops, khaki cotton shirt sleeves rolled up. He smoothed his mustache, observing the faces in the jeep: Across from him sat Armando, a thin-faced Nica-Palestinian, lanky frame crammed into the jeep cab, his long legs folded almost to his chest; Danilo, also a Nica from the States, sported the tattooed initials O. M. on his thickly muscled forearms. A small man in an ill-fitting dark suit, with thinning curly hair, black eyes set deep in his round face, and quietly clasping a blue pocket Bible, rubbed shoulders with Ulises. A plump girl sat crosslegged against the tailgate of the cab; she was about 15 years old, with just-budding breasts and quick eyes; her beige pants had seen better days and her faded blouse had once been a color, maybe yellow. A blond, blue-eyed Swede drove the jeep, and sitting next to him was the stone-faced "responsable" Manuel, who had arranged the rendezvous in San José.

At 5 P.M. that afternoon, Ulises, Armando, and Danilo had appeared at the Parque Nacional in front of the bronze statue commemorating the battle of Rivas in 1856 against William Walker. It

was a Sunday and couples strolled through the park, and it seemed to
Ulises that some people who idled near the statue, smoking cigarettes and killing time, were waiting for the same person. Manuel,
in a blue guayabera, showed up a half-hour late. In his usual curt
manner, he told them a white Toyota jeep was waiting for them a
block away in front of the train station. Ulises noticed Manuel made
contact with 2 other people who quietly slipped away from the park
and headed for the Northern Railroad Station.

The 5 compas crowded into the back of the jeep. Armando and
Danilo kept their heads bent so they wouldn't bang them on the low
roof of the jeep cab. Some brief introductions were exchanged—the
girl's name was Cori, the small man's name was Luis—though it was
just a formality because everyone used pseudonyms, and when you
didn't know someone's pseudonym, you called him compa or compita.

The day before, waiting to make contact with Manuel in a hotel
room in San José, they had chosen their pseudonyms. He'd taken
Ulises, in honor of one who, armed with a rifle and a grenade, had
faced off with a tank in the barrio of Monimbó during the insurrection of September. That Ulises from Masaya had been a warrior-
hero. Though the Ulises who challenged the tank that day had been
killed, his name was now resurrected and would be going into battle
again, carried by a new compa.

Little was said in the jeep, the humming of the engine the only
noise. Ulises thought of the city by the blue bay and saw himself
sitting alone at the bar at Abu Zam Zam's 3 days ago, drinking
amber cognac in that Casablanca setting while old Bruno poured
and discoursed on the decadence and failure that were Ulises's generation. Between filling Ulises's cognacs, Bruno complained heartily of the changes in his little Haight neighborhood brought on by
the drugs and decadence of the flower children. Ulises's peers never
roamed the Haight with flowers in their hair; most of his homeboys
went young in barrio gang wars or in Southeast Asia or rotted in
prisons from Chino to San Quentin. He was the lone survivor of his
barrio who had escaped that triple-threat fate. Those of his generation who survived the protest and drug era now lived unengaged
lives behind a façade of respectability, but still they failed with their
good dreams and good intentions. In the streets of the barrios, vatos

were still killing each other, even more children ran ragged chasing hopeless dreams, and right this minute, no doubt, in the hallowed corridors of the CIA or in the murky depths of Foggy Bottom, some career desk man was surely planning the next Project Phoenix or invasion of the Caribbean or Central America, with all the lost, wasted blood of Nam forgotten. The ones who went to Nam and survived the horror of it were never the same. In other times, the youth of a generation had fought against Fascism in Spain; the young men of his era were asked to kill peasants and rice farmers who didn't even know why they were being slaughtered. As a generation they were decadent, a waste from a moral point of view, that was Bruno's argument, and Ulises figured there might be a gram of truth to it. Maybe that's why Ulises, along with a half-dozen other Chicanos from the Valle and from Los, had come to the front, to salvage the honor of a whole generation who didn't make it. There was no carpet bombing by B-52s here, just people like himself with light arms and automatic weapons trying to kill you and you trying to kill them. He'd always believed that once in your life, without being drafted or impressed, you had to be willing to risk everything for what you believed was righteous, even beautiful, and you had to go to this battle with a pure heart and singing—and this was it for him, a clear-cut, well-defined little war. When a customer asked Bruno's opinion of the great cities of the world, Bruno had answered in his irascible style, "There's only two great cities in the world, San Francisco . . . and Shanghai." Ulises laughed inside at the recollection. He'd had one of those cities, now he didn't know if he'd ever see Shanghai. He'd known many places: sprawling East LA dotted with hills and palm trees, the Manne Hole on Cahuenga where he'd spent many a night listening to greats like Cannonball Adderly wailing saxophone jazz, or at the Lighthouse, feeling the cool blue breezes of the Pacific Ocean; New York, fast and furious, where 5 bucks got you into the Corso to dance all night with the beautiful Puerto Rican women swirling in circles on the dance floor to the bands of Pacheco and Fajardo. Mexico City was greatest once, but now suffocated in mal aires, though he'd always have the Opera Café with its white-coated waiters and its 1920s decor; at the National Palace in the Zócalo, he saw himself in Rivera's murals, in the battle scene where jaguar warriors fought the invading Spaniards.

Chichicastenango was something else—the magic-filled cobble-stone streets, the ancient plaza on market day; he had stood in the church of Santo Tomás bathed in its prismatic light while Indians offered beeswax candles and rose petals to Mayan gods and sacred copal conjured the Popol Vuh—but in the end he had gone back to his barrio by the bay and the one woman that should have always been his—Miriam.

The Swede pulled the jeep over to the side of the road next to a dimly lit food stand. Manuel said they could get out to piss. The 5 hopped out and stretched their legs. They were several hours from the city; the only light was from 3 light bulbs strung in front of the food stand and the cone-shaped headlights of the occasional vehicle passing by. The men relieved themselves against trees; Cori went off into a deeper part of the bush. The Swede, dressed all in white like a milkman, returned with 3 sodas; he handed 2 of them to the back, started the jeep, and drove onto the highway. Manuel pulled a brown paper bag from the glove compartment and withdrew a stack of sandwiches. He handed each of them a wax paper-wrapped sand-wich made of 2 thin slices of bread with an even thinner slice of yellow cheese.

The soft, doughy cheese stuck to the roof of Ulises's mouth like when he was a kid growing up next to the bracero camp and they used to have similar fare for lunch. The 2 sodas were shared, each one taking a swig of syrupy water and passing it on. When they were finished eating and the sodas were empty, Cori recounted the insur-rection of September in Managua, the Open 3 barrio in flames, the streets barricaded, the guardia burning civilian bodies and bombing hospitals. She learned to use a Madzen then and afterwards fled with her family to Costa Rica. Her black eyes burned as she recounted all this with an irrepressible spirit. Then she sang battle songs of the front, getting all of them to follow her lead. The compas crowded in the jeep singing, "¿Cuál es la consigna?" "¿Qué es el FAL?" and "La tumba del guerrillero." Then Cori asked each of them to sing a song, or whatever part they knew. She began by singing "Alforja campe-sina," Ulises tried a few off-key verses of "Bella Ciao," and Armando did "Flor de pino" in a high nasal voice. When they finished all the songs they knew, together they sang "Son tus perjúmenes mujer" till they ran out of verses and Cori started making them up as she went along, "Tus pier-nas son de pavo real. . . ."

* * *

It was past midnight when the jeep left the Pan American Highway and entered the sleeping town of Liberia, lit by the weak street lamps with an eerie yellow light. Ulises, stiff and tired, saw the bandstand in the plaza pass by as the Swede took the jeep into a residential neighborhood street that soon became narrow and paved with cobblestones. The low, tile-roofed houses were set flush to each other, without any yard or fence in between, and their big wooden front doors opened onto the sidewalk. Every few blocks a solitary lightpost cast yellow shadows on the deserted streets. The Swede stopped the jeep in front of a house and Manuel got out and disappeared inside. He returned shortly and everyone followed him in.

The big double wooden doors were closed behind them by a bearded sentry posted inside the house. Two compas with Uzis were on duty inside the large room, bare except for red and black posters of the insurrection on the walls. At the far end of the long room, 2 men and a woman sat behind a large table processing a noisy group of new compas. They waited in this front room till Manuel finished with the responsable of the house. When he was finished, Manuel and the Swede shook hands with them and left.

The 5 of them stepped over to the table where other compas were talking in loud voices. Ulises was the last of his own group to go through the process. A young woman with short brown hair and green fatigues sitting behind the table asked him to empty his pockets and his small Gladstone bag. Ulises set on the table before her a military compass, a red Swiss knife, iodine tablets, a red and black plastic Bic lighter, his notebook, a pencil and a watch. From the Gladstone he pulled out an extra pair of pants, socks, a shirt, and a brown beret, plus a Cuban edition of *El diario del Che en Bolivia*. The picture of Miriam remained in his left shirt pocket.

The compita looked over the material and asked him what kind of tablets they were. "You don't have any identification papers?" she asked.

"I left my passport with Manuel," he answered.

Two men from the other group could be overheard hassling with the compas at the table. The ones arguing were Venezuelans from the Simón Bolívar Brigade that was just entering the front. Ulises didn't understand what the problem was with them. The compita behind the table asked his name, his pseudonym, and where he was from. "So you speak English?"

"Yes, I do," replied Ulises. She wrote all this down, then asked him to go inside and join the rest of his group.

As Ulises gathered his things from the table, the Venezuelans were still arguing. He stepped through a hallway, past a cooking station and out into a large dirt yard where tall deciduous trees and a high wooden fence marked the perimeter. Some 30 compas were sleeping on the ground, using empty rice sacks as blankets. A handful of other compas, also new to the house, stood nearby, carrying their belongings in empty rice sacks.

The responsable of the house came out to meet them. He sported an Australian bush hat and a wispy mustache; a holstered .45 dangled from his hip, the lanyard untied, and his jeans were stuffed inside his calf-high leather boots. He asked all the new compas to fall in. They formed a single file and counted off; there were 10. Danilo was head of the squad. They snapped to attention, then at ease. The responsable addressed them, his hands behind his back, his voice rolling out in the cool night air and entering into every pore of Ulises.

"Compañeros. You will be addressed as compañeros from now on. You are here in a security house. As you well know, the war is raging. We will be sending all of you to a training camp within the next day or 2. In the meantime, you will stay here and train and perform other duties. There's a few things you must get used to right now; you will exercise rigorously to get in top condition. Also, you are not to remove your boots under any circumstances, not even to sleep, understood? A guerrilla must be ready to move at any moment.

"Compañeros, I hope each of you have thought this out carefully, because from here on in, there is no turning back. Once you enter a security house, the only way out is victory or death. You have now passed into a historical position; you are now part of the Southern

Front Benjamín Zeledón. As of this moment, you are under the orders of the General Staff of this house and of this sector. Are there any questions, compañeros? No questions? Then you may turn in for the night. That is all, compas."

The new squad fell out, and the compas picked up 2 or 3 empty rice sacks from a nearby pile. Danilo gave Cori and 2 other compas the first shift on sentry duty inside the security house. The rest of the squad picked out a dry area against a wooden fence to lie down. Ulises tossed his rice sack next to Armando and dropped his Gladstone next to it. Armando was already stretching out on his rice sack. Ulises didn't feel like sleeping just yet.

Luis, in the dark suit, came over to Ulises and asked if he could lie down next to him.

"Sure," Ulises said.

Luis set his bedding down then turned to Ulises; there was something on his mind that he wanted to share. Ulises could see a disturbing emotion on the man's face. Luis, clasping the blue Bible tightly in front of him, started talking as if in midsentence.

". . . I don't know if you're scared, Ulises, but I am, I'm very scared; I feel like I'm going to die. But it doesn't matter. I was praying to God for one thing and he granted it to me. I had been praying that I'd get to see my mother once more, and finally, 3 days ago, I found her in San José. I hadn't seen her in 5 years. She's so old and frail. It was God's will that I should see her one last time, so now if I die, I'll die happy."

Luis had a strange light in his eyes, a distant faraway look as if he was on another plane.

"Do you believe in the Bible, the word of God?" he asked Ulises.

"No, I don't."

"I see," said Luis. "It is all I read; it's the most important book in the world." Ulises didn't respond, but looked hard at the man. Luis wanted to continue, but he saw Ulises wasn't in agreement. Several words stumbled out of his mouth, then he gazed at Ulises and down at his rice sack on the ground, and mumbled something else that Ulises didn't get. Luis turned away from Ulises with hurt feelings and headed for the other side of the yard, perhaps looking for someone else to engage in conversation.

Ulises tried resting on the ground and found the earth cold and hard, with the unique smell of the tropics permeating the yard. He loosened his bootlaces, folded his hands across his stomach, and tried not to think of how uncomfortable he was. He placed his brown beret over his face to keep out the light that was burning in the yard, but he found it impossible to sleep that way—yet Armando was already asleep next to him and other compas around the yard were deep in slumber.

Ulises pulled the beret off his face, crossed his arms behind his head, the annoying light shining in his eyes. So now what? he said to himself, while the words of the responsable swirled in his head. Well now you're in till it's over. For some reason the thought made him panic with doubt that he'd survive. He threw the thought out of his mind, but it left its residue. In his heart he knew that being here was the right thing. Chicano, Mejicano, Nicoya—the same ancient Nahuatl culture and language, the same struggle from Cuauhtemoc to Carlos Fonseca—even if others didn't understand it now, they'd understand it later. And if he did survive this little war? He'd like a crack at film, script a modern version of the myth of Quetzalcoatl and his archnemesis Tezcatlipoca. Set the 2 gods in an urban barrio, make the dieties (without offense) Pachucos, have them speak in street caló, throw in some tropical music—say, Willie Colón and Rubén Blades. Sure, he could make it work; when this was all over, maybe he'd get a chance at that project.

There'd been lots of time once when he could have done everything he ever wanted and more. But so much time had been wasted carousing and storing up experience so that he could say he'd lived, if nothing else. Yeah, he'd lived all right, seriously fast. That reminded him of the time he drove Highway 99 from Lassen to LA; a sudden downpour stopped him in Sacramento and, drying out in the Reno Bar, he met the young chola known as Pinky, who took him to the river where she undressed in the rain, and he had her on the wet, sandy banks of the Sacramento River. He stayed in Sacra a few days; later they drove together to Los Angeles, making it every time they stopped for gas; in the front seat, the back seat, in the fields ripe with strawberries and grapes. Near Delano, they passed a procession of farmworkers led by the image of the Virgen de Guadalupe and a black eagle on a red banner, and he stopped the car and marched with them for miles. Beatrice, the cholita known as Pinky, loved him all the more for it. He was 19 then, the Saint of the San Joaquín, with a black '58 Chevy.

Later there'd been San Francisco, with an endless succession of nights at The Club on Mission Street, dancing rumbas, drinking iced rums, pretty ladies sharing his table. After hours, the all-night parties at the Macondo Club, then with the sun peeking over Potrero Hill, he'd go for breakfast at the Silver Crest where the wide-hipped waitress in the soiled white uniform served him steak and eggs with strong black coffee. Early in the morning when most people were at work, he would stretch his weary bones a few hours on the sofa and be ready to do it all over again that night.

That had been, for sure, the wildest time of his life. He was teaching at the state college and on the weekends he'd drive north to the wine country in his red Triumph TR-3. But most of all, he'd met Miriam, the woman he fell in love with, in what now seemed like a dream of centuries ago. Miriam—he whispered her name to the night and felt the word tremble in his mouth. He reached into his shirt pocket and withdrew the Polaroid photo of a smiling Latin woman with hazel eyes and brown hair. Ulises carried an indelible memory of her lying naked in bed, the early morning sun filtering in through their latticed windows, her small breasts barely covered by the sheets. It was through Miriam that he had met the exiled Nicaraguans—Kike the poet, Willie the pilot, Chombo, and many others—and from them he had first heard of the Front and the struggle against the 45-year reign of the Somozas. One day Kike gave him a letter from Carlos Fonseca, the leader of the Front (typed, probably by Fonseca himself, from somewhere in Nicaragua, with his signature and seal), addressed to the Chicanos in the States, asking for support in the prolonged struggle. Kike had told him then that one day Ulises would be in the mountains, and now here he was, his Georgia boots on and ready. Long before most people in the States had heard of this little country, he was in love with a woman whose mouth tasted of this land, and whose spirit was like the cloud-veiled volcanos rising over the lakes.

A heavy nostalgia filled Ulises. The memories hurt him like a knife twisting in his heart. Miriam—he looked at the face in the photo—whatever possessed you to blame me for the miscarriage? The bitterness of your loss and mine was the beginning of the turbulent months that finally drove us apart. Had we been better able to accept our fate, perhaps we'd still be together in our bed made of love. But in the end I lost you and knew there was no point asking you to wait for me. Who knows if I'll return, or return in one piece? The days before leaving were the loneliest a man could face; you'll never know what a word or a phone call from you would have meant in that monk-like solitude of the hotel room. Now I'm at the front, 3,000 miles away. And you, where are you now? Do other arms hold you and lips kiss you, like I did once? Do you think of someone else now, while I think of you? He didn't want to think of that anymore, it was too painful and he was so far away. He was without a country, without a passport, under another name and there was no turning back. This was his land now, his people, paid with skin, like they say. Che would have said, "Wherever there is struggle, they're my people." That's why out of so many internation-alists at the front, he thought, I must be the only one who gets sentimental about the past—and we all know why they call it the past. He put the photo of Miriam back in his right shirt pocket. He'd always believed that if a man loved a woman completely and totally, without reservations or regrets, she'd always be his. He had loved like that once with Miriam, and he'd lost her anyway. The dull light gleaming in the yard recalled in him the neon nights of the city that were gone forever. He would find it hard to go back to the barrio he'd known, and if he did, who would remember his name? or what he once did there? or what he'd done since? The last bit of nostalgia fluttered haplessly like a wayward moth as it left him, leaving in its place the rolling drum-voice of the responsable echoing in his head in counterpoint to the distant, long-ago merengue that Guillén's band closed The Club with every night,

> A la rigola yo no vuelvo más,
> Matan los hombres en la madrugá'
> Matan los hombres en la madrugá'!

Morning Light

It was around 0300 hours and still dark when Ulises, Armando, and Danilo, along with 5 other compas, were woken up during their first night at the security house. The 8 compas and 2 responsables filed out to the deserted street and the 2 waiting Volkswagen vans; "a special mission" was all they were told. The vans took a zigzag route; no one could really tell where they were going because the windows were curtained so they couldn't see outside. No one said much, they just sat sleepily in the vans not knowing what they were setting out to do.

The vans drove all over Liberia for half an hour or so, then pulled off to the side of the road and stopped. The driver killed the engine and said they were going to wait here for a while. A couple of compas lit cigarettes while they waited.

An hour must have gone by, then they continued again. In 15 minutes the vans started slowing down, then halted. The van doors swung open and the compas got out. They were on an asphalt strip. It was still dark, but lights were burning inside a small hangar. Outside the hangar doors stood a couple of 4-seater planes. Two big canvas-topped trucks were parked on the opposite side of the strip. First light hadn't broken and the muggy heat was already stifling.

In a few minutes someone by the trucks started shouting, "¡Ya viene! It's coming, it's coming!"

Ulises, standing by the vans gazing at the purple heavens, saw 4 tiny lights appear in the southern sky, then heard the roar of the engines as the plane began its descent to the runway. A DC-8 4-prop cargo plane, all silver streamlined and without markings, touched

Alejandro Murguía

down with a thump, went to the end of the runway, then turned back and taxied up to the 2 trucks.

Ulises and the other compas ran to the plane as the trucks lined up at the 2 port entrances and the cargo doors swung wide open. An assembly line was formed for each truck; 2 compas in the plane, 2 between the plane and the truck ramp, and 2 more compas under the canvas top. The belly of the plane was loaded with heavy wooden crates stamped Fabrique d'Armes Léger-Belgique. Fourteen FALs to a crate and each FAL 10 pounds. And plenty of crates full of 7.62 NATO-type ammunition for the FALs. The compas didn't mind the hard and heavy work when they saw what they were unloading. A good 75 crates later, the sweat poured down Ulises's face, and his arms and legs were trembling.

Finally the hold of the plane was empty and the 2 trucks were loaded, so the compas got back in the vans as the trucks left for the front and the plane prepared for takeoff. They all felt pretty good, and the first rays of dawn were just beginning to peek above the distant mountains. A Civil Guard sentry in blue uniform at the gate exit of the airport stopped their driver and made a cursory inspection of their van.

Ulises was sitting in there with Armando, Danilo, and another compa, smoking, sweaty, and tired. And the Civil Guard said to them as he waved the driver through,

"Buena suerte, muchachos."

To the Front

"We started the offensive by routing the guardia from El Naranjo, then we went into El Ostional. The plan was to take a back road into Rivas and cut off the southern part of the country. Our squad leader told us to leave all our heavy gear behind, but I refused; I brought everything along. Even carried a little shovel for days that the squad leader kept telling me to get rid of. But I held on to it. Then we ran out of water and everyone was going crazy 'cause we didn't have water for 2 days. I brought out my little shovel and scraped a small hole in some muddy ground and water seeped in. I told the compas, 'Look, it's water. It may not be fresh, but it's water. Scoop some up.' And everyone did, including the squad leader. He never hassled me again about the shovel. It was a mistake going into El Ostional and El Naranjo, 'cause it was just hill country and there was nothing of importance that could be held. Then a fierce storm broke and we bogged down at El Ostional. We were wet to the bone all the time. Slept in trenches 2 feet deep in water. It was a matter of enduring 'cause we weren't going anywhere. The guardia hit us with 500-pound bombs, push-pulls and everything else. It became impossible to stay there, so it was decided to regroup and attack Peñas Blancas. It was still raining when the order came to pull out. Our withdrawal turned into a disaster when the guardia spotted our movement and fell on us with everything they had. I was in the rear guard when a compa next to me was picked off with a Galil. *Piiing.* Here, below the right eye. The compa cried out, 'Ayy! They've hit me,' and fell dead at my feet. All I could do was take his rifle to keep it from falling into the guardia's hands. We lost a lot of good compas in that retreat in the rain from El Ostional."

Norman finished and stared blindly at the empty brown beer bottles that covered the surface of the round table. Ulises and the Panamanian, Morales, had a girl sitting between them; she smoked while they drank beers.

"More beer!" Norman demanded suddenly of no one in particular.

Ulises eyed the girl next to him, her plain face smiling under her short haircut, her white blouse half buttoned in an inviting V. Morales, black beret perched on his fluffy afro, took another swig and said nothing as the girl's friend returned to join them at the table. The combo on stage kept up the raggedy beat as 3 couples danced listlessly across the sawdust floor.

Norman pinned Ulises with a hard stare of his reddened eyes.

"You," he pointed at Ulises, "Tomorrow I'm taking you to the front with me. My brother has a squad on the line at Sapoá. He'll take good care of us."

"You know I haven't been to camp yet?"

"Where were you before they moved you to my place?"

"Doing duty at a security house outside of town."

"That's all right. I'll teach you to break down the FAL. After a few lessons on how to throw yourself under fire, you'll feel like a veteran. The thing is to keep your heels flat so the shrapnel won't hit you. Of course, if you want to leave the front, that's an easy way out. Bam! A little shrapnel on the heel, and you're out."

"Maybe I should pass through the training camp first."

"Why? You're not afraid, are you?"

"Would I be here if I was?" Ulises responded.

"Good, that's the talk I like. Welcome to the raffle. Now how about some more beers? You have money, ¿que no?"

"A little."

"Well, let's have it, man. It's the last night before going to the front. Let's make a night of it."

Ulises reached into his jeans pocket and pulled out a green bill folded many times into a small square. Carefully he unfolded it, smoothed it out, then handed it to Norman.

"What? Ten American dollars is all you have?"

"That's it," replied Ulises.

Morales said to them, "Puma had 300 American dollars that he got from Panamá. And he only gave me 5. 300! ¡Dólares! ¡Americanos! I couldn't believe it."

"I thought you had more than this," said Norman. "Have you been lying, or what? If I'd known this was all you had, I would've been home an hour ago."

"What makes you think I have money?" Ulises asked, getting irritated by Norman's line of questioning.

"All you gringos are rich, no? Ha, ha." Norman stood up, hands on hips, legs wide and firmly planted, and looked around the cabaret at the couples sharing beers in the dark corners, as if challenging someone—anyone—to say something to him. When no one noticed him, Norman went off to the bar with Ulises's 10-dollar bill. Ulises finished the rest of his beer in one gulp and set the empty bottle down hard on the table.

Morales pulled his chair over to Ulises and said in a confidential tone, "You know the girls want us to walk them home. They live nearby."

"All right, then what?"

"Well, this one likes me. Maybe she'll let me stay."

Ulises was silent.

Then Morales spilled out, "Not much of a chance, really. She said they're at our table 'cause they know we're going to the front. Tica women aren't like the ones in Panamá. Our women are really hot."

Norman returned with his arms full of beers, which he spread out among them, pushing aside the empties. He placed a cold, foamy bottle in front of Ulises. Ulises didn't touch it.

"Say, Norman." Ulises didn't hide the belligerent tone in his voice. "I may be from the States, but when did you ever see a gringo who looked like me?"

"Don't take it so seriously. But you did say you were from up there, didn't you?"

"What about it? My family also comes from México."

"Forget it. It was a stupid joke. You have to admire the internationalists, we all do. And thank you for your help. I have heard though that there is a gringo at the front. A chele, I don't know."

"Neither do I," said Ulises. "I've met some West Germans, like that girl Ulla, but that's it."

Ulises clicked bottles with the group—Morales next to him, the girl with short hair, the plump one with the pretty face, and Norman. Norman threw his head back and chugged the beer, foam spilling down his chin. The house combo of the Sirena Encantadora took a break, setting aside their instruments and standing up at the bar. Two of the girls at the club gathered around the musicians. Morales turned his attention to the girl next to him, engaging her in close conversation while Norman placed his hand over the plump hand of the other girl. Ulises was thinking he'd drunk enough beer; his thoughts were spinning like the colored lights swirling in the room. Whether they walked the girls home or not, he would have to return to the security house with Norman, and Morales would go to the house where the Pana volunteers were billeted. Norman would go to sleep with his wife, 6 months pregnant, and the rest of the house would be taken up with compas recuperating from wounds. But Ulises and 2 other compas would sleep in the back yard in a chicken coop. He could fall asleep anywhere now, and the coop was cozier than sleeping in the mud, but it was sleeping alone. He didn't want to start thinking of the girls at the table. He took another drink, brooding on what Norman had said. On one hand, Norman was an all right guy; as responsable of the security house, he let them out for the weekend, even gave them some colones. Yet, sometimes Norman could be a pain. He decided that Norman was drunk and he wouldn't think of his remarks anymore. Ulises was an internationalist and he'd been all over—México, Guatemala, Panamá, now Nicaragua. He knew some routes. Everything in his past seemed so distant from this perspective; his family, did they suspect? And Miriam? In the process of forgetting him by now, no doubt. That's what happens when you're gone and no one knows when or if you're coming back. Shit, he thought, you made your choice, took your chances. Couldn't stay on the sidelines while young people were being massacred by the score in León and Masaya, or while Somoza bombed Estelí to rubble, like Franco did Guernica. He took another swig of suds and knew he had no regrets about losing any of what he had lost.

Morales stood up, his chocolate face shiny, swaying unsteadily. With one hand on the girl's shoulder for support, he raised his arms and asked for silence from Norman and attention from the rest.

"The famous Panamanian tango singer, Pepe 'Gardel' Morales, will now sing one of his biggest hits. Maestro," he said, motionin to an invisible orchestra, "whenever you're ready!"

Morales threw his head back, closed his eyes as if he was on stage, and held his arms stiffly at his side. The whirling mirrored ball that spun on the ceiling of the Sirena Encantadora reflected 1,000 tiny fragments of light on his face as he began to sing an ancient tango of nostalgic return.

> Yo adivino el parpadeo
> de las luces que a lo lejos
> van marcando mi retorno . . .

*   *   *

Near midnight, a dark green jeep took the back roads out of Liberia till it hit the main highway, then headed north to the Nicaraguan border. After an hour or so of travel, the jeep turned off the main highway and onto a narrow dirt road. They bumped along the dirt road till they came to a split-rail fence. The driver got out to open the gate, then continued on the road till they came to a 2-story, wood-frame ranch house. The large rooms of the ranch house were empty except for several MAG machine guns with tripods. Ulises slept on the floor, stretched out on empty rice sacks. In Liberia he'd left the Gladstone at Norman's house and bought a small green knapsack that he used now as a pillow. At daybreak the next morning they left the farmhouse on foot, crossing a meadow still wet with dew, with 9 compas in a single file—the 7 just come from Liberia and 2 guides. Strapped high on their backs were provision-stuffed backpacks they had each been given before leaving the ranch house. They crossed through several barbed-wire fences and more meadows, and kept going till they came to a swiftly running river. The river was wide and about 2 feet deep. They plunged forward, stepping on rocks that peaked above the current as the river swirled at times up to their thighs and filled their boots with icy water.

When they were across the river, they rested on the pebbly banks for 5 minutes before continuing their march. On this side of the river the ground was hilly and covered with tall coniferous trees. Their guide led them up a steep, rocky, muddy hillside and they struggled with their backpacks, adjusting them on their backs as they climbed. Ulises could see that there were several trails leading toward the hilltop. Near the peak of the hill they came into a bald clearing under a canopy of giant trees whose branches embraced like long-lost lovers, blocking out the sun and the sky above.

Ulises's first impression was that there was utter chaos and confusion in the camp; a swarm of compas ran about very busily, some unarmed, some armed with a variety of weapons. There were Belgian FALs, ancient Garands, Israeli Galils, and U.S.-made M-1 carbines and M-16s. Then he noticed that deeper in the foliage where it hadn't been trampled or chopped down, there were many tents made of black plastic sheets hung over twine stretched between 2 branches or trunks. Between the large trees there was much brush—bushes, smaller trees, and saplings. Their guide led them through the confusion to the center of camp.

Four men with .45s strapped to the hip, 2 of them with M-1s, issued orders to a group of compas who dashed off. Their guide introduced the 4 compas. Diego, tall, sallow-complexioned, limping from a leg wound, with a brown beret and an M-1. El Viejo, a grizzled veteran, with a stubbly white beard and a black beret cocked on his head. Harold, from the column José Benito Escobar, and Eduardo, the comandante of the camp, in razor-sharp fatigues and tightly fitting olive green T-shirt, a .45 tight at his waist. This was the General Staff of the camp.

"Show them where they'll be camped," Eduardo told the guide, who marched them off.

Before following the rest, Ulises greeted Eduardo.

"¿Qué tal, Eduardo, remember me?"

Eduardo squinted. "Yes. I remember."

"The Solidarity Committee sends you greetings."

"Thanks. What have you heard of Kike?" Eduardo asked.

"He's in the States now, organizing the takeover of the consulates. Have you seen Armando? He was with another Nica, Danilo."

"Yes, Danilo left for the front immediately. Armando 3 days ago. You better catch up with your squad. I'll talk to you later."

Ulises ran off to join his squad. The last time he'd seen Eduardo was after the insurrection of September. He'd met him in a restaurant outside San José on the road to Cartago. Eduardo was sick and haggard that day; he'd just come out of the front with intestinal problems. Ulises gave him money and vitamins that he had on him. The Eduardo that Ulises now found in charge of the training camp "El Pelón" was very different. This Eduardo looked mean, hungry, and was clean-shaven; he barked out orders with the intensity of a drill sergeant.

The squad spent the rest of the day carving out a niche for itself, building 2 plastic tents that would billet the 10 compas that the squad had grown to. In the afternoon, Eduardo came by carrying a black FAL. He asked the squad to fall into formation, single file. Another compa with Eduardo shouldered 2 Garands. Eduardo addressed the squad.

"Compitas, you're going to the firing range with compa Miguel here to learn to use the FAL and the Garand. While you're in camp only the squad leaders carry armament." He looked over the 10 compas lined up, arms at their sides. He saw Ulises and told him to step forward.

"Here," Eduardo said, tossing Ulises the FAL chest-high.

Ulises caught the heavy FAL and clutched it tightly.

"Take the squad with Miguel," Eduardo said.

Miguel started off and Ulises fell in behind him. The rest of the squad followed single file down the hilltop heading for the next series of hills where the firing range was hidden.

*   *   *

Ulises and the Spaniard stepped carefully over the slippery rocks that pitted the side of the hill nearest the river. Thick trees covered the camp on the hilltop. They were going down to the river to wash the squad's plastic plates. The angle was steep and rocky where they squatted pachuco style, a cuclillas, at the river's edge. The water rushed swiftly over the smooth rocks. Ulises laid the black FAL on dry ground between the Spaniard and himself and dipped the plastic dishes into the foamy water. The heavy, violent FAL—christened

Miriam, in her honor—was now his constant companion, the last thing he saw when he fell asleep and his wake-up reminder every sunrise.

Ulises ran his hand over the 100 little nicks scratched on the plastic bottoms of the plates, a tiny gouge left by each compa who had stabbed at his ration of rice with the controlled fury of the truly hungry. Other groups of compas were gathered along the river bank rinsing the dishes for the squads hidden in the hilltop.

"So what did you do in Spain?" Ulises asked.

"I was a history teacher in high school. I've always been political; I used to belong to a party."

"What made you decide to come?"

"It was something I'd been debating inside for a long time. But I had a contract with the school and I didn't think it was right to break my word. So when the contract expired I left."

"What's your pseudonym?"

The Spaniard laughed, "What else? Gaspar."

"Good choice," Ulises said. "The original Gaspar's pseudonym was Martín. They say the men who were with him cried when he was killed."

"I guess everyone in the Southern Front has heard of the Spanish priest, Gaspar García Laviana. He must have been a unique man," the Spaniard said.

"He's become a legend, really. He was also a poet. He fell in an ambush; they say he was betrayed by an oreja among the campesinos."

"And what did you do?"

"I've done everything from being a teacher to driving buses."

"What made you decide to come?"

"I belonged to a committee that was working in the solidarity movement. The committee has sent about 20 compas down here. I'm one of them."

When the dishes were finished, they stacked them and carried them back up the hill, careful not to slip on the rocks. As they climbed, the rocks gave way to brush and then the trees got thicker. The ground was muddy from recent rains, and the grass and weeds that grew there were trampled down. At the top of the hill they came to a clearing under a thick canopy of trees. The place had seemed like chaos when Ulises first arrived, but now after 2 days he understood the rhythm and had no trouble feeling the pulse of the camp.

Ulises and Gaspar crossed the clearing near the tents of the General Staff. El Viejo, the grizzled veteran, was lecturing some 20 new recruits.

"This is a training camp for riflemen," El Viejo was saying. "If anyone told you different, they're wrong. In the few days you'll be here, we'll try to give you as much help as we can. You will not be going into a hit-and-run guerrilla war; you will be entering a front where a war of positions is taking place. You will be expected to hold your ground."

Same thing he said to us, thought Ulises, as they went past El Viejo and the new recruits. Ulises and Gaspar kept going till they reached the black plastic tents at the edge of the camp.

Gaspar went off to return the dishes while Ulises inspected the 2 tents where the squad was billeted. Cleto, the bony Black Nica from Corn Island, had done a fine job setting up the tents. Each of the tents could fit 5 or 6 compas. A main line was strung between 2 tree trunks, a black plastic sheet folded over, then each corner of the sheet was staked down to secure it. A little ditch ran around each tent to drain off the water in case of rain. From inside one of the tents, Ulises could hear Radio Reloj announcing the news. The fighting was going well in León and Estelí, Ezequiel's column had Rivas under siege, in Managua where the fighting was fiercest, it seemed to be a standoff. Ulises recalled the time on the freighter off the Florida Keys when he heard the radio reports of the East LA riots and the death of Rubén Salazar.

Before Gaspar returned to the tents, the call went out through the camp. "Formation!"

Everyone dropped what they were doing and scrambled to line up with their squads. One hundred fifty recruits were running frantically, jumping over bushes, running into each other, picking up gear and carrying it in their arms like babies; locating their squads and getting everyone to line up at attention, while through the camp came the booming voice of Eduardo counting off 23-24-25, timing how long it took for the camp to jump into formation.

All the squads fell in, each squad having 10 compas. Eduardo counted till he reached 80 before he was satisfied that the squads were at attention. Fifteen squads lined up, eyes straight ahead, under the diffused light of the pine grove. The recruits all wore civilian clothes, except that here and there someone was wearing a red and black scarf or a beret; some wore olive green T-shirts, some had boots, some didn't. A few wore the baggy pants of civilians; some wore jeans. It's an army of students and teachers, of workers and those without work, of women and men, thought Ulises.

All eyes in the camp faced forward while Eduardo pinned the whole camp down with his cold-eyed stare, his hands on his waist, his elbows out, his neck forward.

"Are the new recruits of the Southern Front ready for calisthenics?" barked Eduardo.

The entire camp responded in one booming voice.

"YES, COMPAÑERO!"

"Good. Then let us begin."

Eduardo led them through a series of exercises, doing each one of them himself. The session ended with 80 deep knee bends, one for each second it had taken the camp to fall in, with arms stretched out in front and the squad leaders with their heavy FALs held out front, and the whole camp going down and up. When they finished, Ulises's legs were tight and trembling. Then Eduardo made an announcement.

"Compañeros. There has been a change of plan. Due to an unforeseen emergency in this sector, we have received orders to break camp and evacuate everyone here. That means all of you will be leaving for the front tonight. You can start breaking down the tents now, and be prepared to move after nightfall. That is all."

Eduardo turned around and left with the camp General Staff. The squads broke up in an excited buzz, everyone talking at once and asking questions. Cleto spoke up.

"I heard on the radio that a camp had been spotted by OAS aircraft. Maybe it was this one."

"Could be," answered Ulises. "You all heard the comandante; let's grab our gear, break the tents down, and be ready to move."

Ulises looked at the faces in his squad. There was Fredy, a square-faced, big-boned 15-year-old Nica, jailed and beaten by the guardia. Eddy, not much older, just out of high school. Charley, a

Tico-Nica from Costa Rica with dark puppy eyes, about 22. Quincho from Matagalpa. Malek, an Arab-Nica from Bluefields with thick horn-rimmed glasses perched on his nose, who had dropped out of the university in San José to join the front. And black Cleto from Corn Island, the only one with any experience, having led the takeover of Corn Island armed with a .38. The rest were internationalists: Ernesto, a blond chele from Colombia; Dany, a short, mean-faced Tico from the streets of San José; Gaspar, the Spaniard; and himself. Too many kids and not much experience in the squad, thought Ulises.

"Any questions?" he asked.

There were none, so Ulises set the squad to dismantling the 2 tents, and when they finished, the compas stayed nearby, smoking and talking, or just sitting quietly under the trees.

The camp grew quiet as night fell through the pines. Word filtered through the camp for the squads to line up; they were formed into 2 columns and 1 platoon. Harold named Ulises head of the platoon. First in line was the column Miguel Enríquez, followed by Ulises's platoon, then the column José Benito Escobar. When there was total darkness, the compas formed into one long column that snaked through the pines, moving downhill toward the river and the open meadows.

There was no light in the pine grove, and the squads moved through the shadows like kelp drifting in an open sea. The squads of the column Miguel Enríquez were already descending the hilltop; Ulises and Gaspar had the platoon ready to move when a commotion in the column José Benito Escobar broke out. It began with a shouting that grew louder and fiercer till it swept through the hilltop in undulating waves. As the shouting grew louder and more disruptive, everyone's attention became focused on the tail end of the column where the commotion was centered. The movement of the column stalled as compas' attention wandered toward what was happening in the José Benito Escobar, and slowly everyone was drawn there.

The problem centered around a handful of men in the rear of the column. As Ulises approached the ring of compas, the intensity of emotions was like a tightly wound spring about to snap. The circle rapidly expanded as compas gathered around; 2 compas with flashlights pointing down were in the center of the ring. Between them stood a tired-faced man with cutoff jeans and a striped shirt that Ulises had seen on cleanup details around the camp. Next to this threesome, Harold, a member of the camp General Staff, was haranguing the column and waving his M-1 up and down. The light reflected from the flashlights cast an eerie glow on the 4, distorting their features and giving the scene the aura of a horror movie.

The circle expanded and grew as more compas fell out of line and gathered around the disturbance. Ulises stood lost in the crowd as Harold drove them to hysteric intensity, urging them to respond to his badgering.

"For the traitors!"

"¡Paredón!"

Ulises didn't know why Harold was asking for the execution of this man, but it was obvious that he had many compas on his side. Ulises noticed there were some like himself who weren't shouting "paredón." Eduardo suddenly appeared in the circle and asked what was going on. Harold responded loudly enough for everyone to hear.

"This son-of-a-whore," he said, pointing to the man in cutoff jeans, "tried to escape from camp tonight. Our security forces caught him on his way out. Now what do you think he was going to do?" Harold asked the attentive crowd, then answered his own question. "This bastard was going to inform on the whereabouts of this camp!"

"¡Paredón! ¡Paredón!" The shouting picked up and gathered momentum, rustling the leaves on the trees. Ulises gripped the thick stock of the FAL tightly. Eduardo raised his arms for silence.

"Compañeros. We all know the penalty for desertion is very hard. But we must give him a chance to explain his actions. You, what do you have to say?"

The man looked at the crowd like a fox trapped by baying hounds. His eyes revealed total fear, and he glanced down and spoke to the ground.

"I didn't like it here. So I wanted to leave. That's all. I wasn't going to reveal anything."

"¡Paredón! ¡Paredón! ¡Paredón!"

"Silence, compañeros!" Eduardo shouted. "We are at war here. We cannot afford infiltrators or traitors. At the same time, we must deal with this quickly and effectively. But there is an option. There is an island where we keep top security prisoners of war. This man could be sent there. We'll have to decide now under wartime conditions. If you believe he should be executed, say so. If you think he should be sent to prison on the Island of Coiba, then say it." Eduardo looked over at Harold, who returned him a look of contempt.

Harold raised his M-1.

"Those who think he should get what he deserves."

Half the camp exploded in triple shouts of "¡Paredón!" Then Eduardo spoke.

"Those who think he should be imprisoned at Coiba."

An amount equal to half or more shouted, "¡Coiba! ¡Coiba!" Eduardo decided.

"He'll go to Coiba till the war is over, then we'll deal with him." And to the guards he said, "Take him away and turn off those lamps." In the sudden quiet and darkness of the grove he ordered, "Everyone back to your places. Let's move!"

Everyone scrambled back to position among their squads and columns. Then began the slow descent from the hill, the columns moving forward and bunching up and moving forward again under the cover of trees and night. The column stumbled along in the mud; someone slipped somewhere in front and Ulises could hear the thud and the curses that followed. The column halted, then started up again. Ulises carried the FAL slung over his right shoulder and his knapsack on his back.

When they came out from under the trees, a full and vibrant moon in a cloudless sky illuminated the countryside of rolling hills. A river like a glittering silver snake cut through the landscape, and the moonlight revealed the swirls and currents they would have to cross. Half the column was stretched out in a single file down the hillside and was approaching the near bank. Small, round hills dotted the far side of the river, and beyond that were the flatlands and meadows. The river was the same one they had crossed coming into camp, the same one where they had bathed and washed dishes. Ulises gripped the FAL by the steel barrel and balanced it horizontally on his shoulder to keep it above the water. He stepped into the cold, knee-high current and hadn't gone more than a few steps when he slipped on a mossy rock and went down to his chest. He quickly jerked the FAL higher and pulled himself up out of the river. He managed to save the FAL but that was it. He was thoroughly soaked and his knapsack was gushing water. Jaw knotted with rage, he cursed his clumsiness and continued across. When the 2 columns finished crossing the river, the dust stuck to Ulises's pant legs, turning to mud. The march continued a few more kilometers till they came to a meadow near the old farmhouse where they had slept the first night. By then Ulises was shivering in his damp clothes, but there was nothing he could do about it.

On the dirt road that led to the farmhouse, 4 big canvas-topped trucks were waiting. The columns lined up in squad formation while the General Staff made one final review of squad after squad, lit by a brilliant full moon hanging wistfully in a star-studded sky. Before boarding the trucks, the comandantes of the columns addressed the waiting compas. Then the peacefulness of the country night was split open by the deafening roar of 150 compas, fists raised in the air, shouting as one with all the fervor in their souls so it could be heard in the bunker of the dictator,

"LONG LIVE THE FRENTE SANDINISTA!"
"LONG LIVE THE HEROS AND MARTYRS!"
"THE POPULAR SANDINISTA INSURRECTION WILL TRIUMPH!"
"¡PATRIA LIBRE!"
"¡O MORIR!"

                              *   *   *

A small triangular patch of purple firmament peeked through a tear in the canvas top of the truck heading for the front. A single star in that bit of universe sent its light streaming into Ulises's upturned eyes. Under the canvas top of the truck, the compas stood shoulder to shoulder, the rumbling of the 6-wheeler vibrating up through their feet and into their bones. Ulises could only see the distant star through the hole in the canvas, the shadowy forms of other compas and the profile of Gaspar next to him; the FAL rubbed against his hip and his wet clothes kept him shivering with cold.

The journey to the border was immeasurable in time and distance. It could have been 10 kilometers or 2 hours, hidden in the belly of the truck, covered by the black tarp, indistinguishable from any other truck on the highway. Could anyone seeing the 4-truck caravan passing guess what was inside? Ulises wondered how he would react under fire. His grandfather had fought in the Mexican Revolution; an aunt on his father's side, one-time homecoming queen of Jalisco, had died of malaria nursing the wounded of Madrid during the Spanish Civil War; his uncle Agustín on his mother's side survived a sniper's bullet on Iwo Jima; his older brother earned a Silver Star during the Tet Offensive and later a Purple Heart; Armando tasted the insurrection of September and Danilo had seen Nam—but he'd been left behind when they went to the front. Now he was following the same road. Ulises could run 5 miles uphill, do 40 push-ups on his knuckles, spar 3 rounds, assemble an M-1 blindfolded, hit the bull's-eye at 100 meters. He was as ready as he was ever going to be. As ready as Toño would have wanted him to be. Toño, the 19-year-old Nica who passed briefly through the States, inspiring many of them with his discipline and morale. Toño, ex-student of Garfield High in East LA, homeboy, the military hero in the takeover of Rivas the year before who'd led the assault squad at Peñas Blancas armed with a bazooka. Toño now dead. Ulises recalled Cori's chubby face and asked himself why a 15-year-old girl should be going to war. In Liberia he'd met the 14-year-old who'd captured Lt. Buitrago at Los Mojones; the kid was already a veteran with wounds to heal. Damn, how could anyone sit on their rear while this was going on? How could he face himself 10 years later if he didn't do something now? Shit, he was 29; if he had to go, this was as good a time as any.

The starlight disappeared as the truck passed under a thick net of branches. The trucks came to a halt. Inside the canvas top the air turned hot and muggy. Cranking chains brought the back gate down; the tarp was lifted, letting in cool, breezy air. One by one the compas jumped out the back, landing with a squat on the hard asphalt road. The moon had been covered by a mantle of clouds; a low mist hugged their feet searching for the ground. Only shadows moved among shadows.

As Ulises's eyes got used to the dark, he could make out the square block forms of buildings along the highway. Out of the black ink of the shadows, compas appeared with rifles strapped across their chests, floppy jungle hats pulled low. The 2 columns were formed,

Ulises's platoon at the head of them, and led to a nearby abandoned building with a long, sloping roof and many windows. Giant guanacaste trees surrounded the buildings and a heavy, ominous silence filled the stagnant air.

The 150 men and women in the columns were led single file beside the stucco walls and concrete landing of the abandoned Costa Rican customs building. The border with Nicaragua was 500 meters away. Ulises was at the point of the columns nearest the border. He placed the FAL between himself and Gaspar and used his knapsack and beret as a pillow to rest his head. His back against the concrete, Ulises ran his hand down the smooth stock of the FAL named Miriam. No one knew what the morning would bring; Ulises closed his eyes and fell into a deep sleep.

His sleep was filled with disturbing dreams of the past. Miriam appeared just beyond his outstretched arms, talking to him in that strange dream way, but he couldn't quite hear, so she came closer and closer, Ulises reaching for her with open arms.

The bright white flash of a mortar explosion twenty meters away and the dull metallic BAHGON! sound of the shock wave hit him simultaneously, slamming his eyes open and shaking the branches of the trees above. The blast shook everyone up. Gaspar reached out a hand to touch him. "You all right, Ulises?"

"Yes, I'm all right." He didn't say his heart was beating 100 miles an hour. He was stunned by how loud the explosion had been, and found himself short of breath, his heart beating rapidly. It took him a moment to recover and become fully awake from the dream. Then he felt something odd. Putting his right hand down his pants, he felt the stickiness in his groin. Jesus, he thought, I just had a wet dream. My God, how long's it been? He withdrew his moist fingers. It was the dream of Miriam, at the same time as the explosion. A sudden rush of sadness and nostalgia overpowered him and swirled around in the hollow ringing left after the explosion. Every emotion he'd ever felt about Miriam came at him, confusing and disturbing, changing his equilibrium to chaos, and with the driftwood from the past came a crazy, irrational fear that made him feel like running away, hiding in the dark hills or hitchhiking out on the highway.

With the quieting of the leaves, the smell of burnt gunpowder drifted over to them. Ulises could feel the tautness of the compas in the column. His own senses became finely tuned and hypersensitive to his surroundings. He could have picked out the crawling of an ant on a leaf above. Gaspar, stretched out rigid as a board, glanced over at Ulises. "Do you think they'll keep hitting us?"

Ulises remembered something that Che had said in the diary.

"There's nothing you can do about it," he answered. "The chances of a direct hit by a mortar are very slim. So why worry? Best thing would be to get some sleep."

"You can sleep through this?"

"Have to. Don't want to waste energy; might need it in the morning."

A sigh escaped Gaspar's lips and he lay back down. The landscape was still; with it came the tenseness of waiting for the next shell to fall. Ulises turned on his side, his head on the knapsack, his hands covering his face, the black FAL resting at his side like the woman who used to sleep next to him.

The booming of mortars started again. The white phosphorus flash of the explosions was landing far away, followed a few seconds later by the hollow metal thud of the sound wave. The fire line was moving away from them. Ulises propped himself up on one elbow and watched the fireballs landing on a distant hill. The first explosion had shocked him, sent his heart racing; now the beat was steady and calm, and he'd gotten over the shock. But at that first instant of the explosion his life had flashed before him and he felt lucky to have seen it all go by so fast. It was only supposed to happen when you were dying; shame left no heirs—once with Miriam, almost. It'd be strange to see her again, should he ever return . . . how would she feel about him? No answers to the questions . . . he knew he couldn't sleep now; it was nearing 0500 hours. The approaching whine of a solitary shell came tearing through the treetops and he covered his head with his arms as the projectile landed not far from where the first one had exploded. The shrapnel tore the leaves above him into shreds. Gaspar sat upright as if wanting to bolt.

"Stay down," Ulises said, "Don't make yourself a target."

Gaspar lay down again. Ulises, at the point of the column, the echo of the barrage sounding in his ears, knew now he would not run, he would hold his ground when the time came, and with the cold calm of the warrior, he waited for daybreak on the border.

Front Line

"At Peñas Blancas we hit the guardia barracks with recoilless rifles in the middle of the night. When the smoke cleared, the guardia had abandoned the town and compas were swarming all over the duty-free stores, the restaurants, and everything. It was like a movie, with compas sporting expensive sunglasses and toting imported whiskies looted from the dictators' own stores. We kept after the guardia and hit them again in Sapoá with the columns of the Batallón de Combate Gaspar García Laviana, and advanced all that night and the next day till we came to this river. Here we had to halt.

"On the other side of the river there's just flat land, a farmhouse, and Hill 50. In flat terrain like this where one sniper can stop a whole column, you advance with your balls in your hand. You can't see the farmhouse from here, but that's where Comandante Roger got hit. We'd been taking a lot of artillery fire and our own stuff was going wide, landing up by the lake. So the comandante was in the farmhouse directing fire when a shrapnel tore through his throat, killing him instantly. You get used to those artillery duels; they hit us for a while, then we hit them.

"It's kinda quiet now, so you're all right. But the aviation will come by soon, then all you can do is hug the earth and pray to your mother. Yesterday a helicopter dropped a 500-pound bomb on Sapoá, killing 4 compas. The shock wave from one of those babies can pick you up and slam you down like you were a bean bag, follow me? So when they start pounding us with the big ones, hit the dirt flat as you can and keep your mouth open so the concussion won't burst your eardrums. That's another thing. Dig yourself a good trench. Nice and deep. And when it rains you'll get up to your armpits in water. But you'll live. That's the important thing. I'm not like those guys who go around taking chances. Not me. I stay crouched down, hopping from trench to trench. You know, some compas risk going all the way to Sapoá for hot coffee. I do without. Why take the chance of getting hit over a cup of coffee?

"See those trees across the river? You have to watch them all the time 'cause the guardia likes to sneak snipers in there with telescopic sights. Plenty of compas have gotten it that way. Sometimes the guardia comes at us all hopped up on pills, their mouths foaming, eyes wild; you have to pop them a few times to stop them. Don't worry about being scared—everyone is. Whoever says he's not scared is a liar. The thing is to control your fear and not let it control you. Your chances get better after the first few days, but if you worry about getting killed, you *will* get killed. If you can survive the first day or 2, you'll make it. Yesterday, for instance, they sent a new man up here. It was his first day at the front, just like you, and he was very nervous and scared. He was a trained artillery spotter and he went and took a position on that little mound you see over there. Well, I swear he hadn't been there 10 minutes when a mortar landed right where he'd stationed himself. Poof, a cloud of dust and he was gone. Hadn't been at the front 10 minutes. See what I mean?"

Squad Leader

The sound of the light airplane sent the 2 guerrillas scrambling off the edge of the tree-lined highway, down through bramble shrubs that grew thick along a creek's embankment, till they came to where the water ran clear and cold over smooth rocks. The squad leader carried a Belgian-made FAL slung over one shoulder, a backpack, and 5 clips on his web belt. His uniform was olive green fatigues and a black beret, his round face was burned by the sun and showed traces of smallpox scars. At El Naranjo he had been in a squad where only 3 survived; now he led his own squad entrenched on the banks of the Río Ostallo. The other man was a new recruit. His features had the sculptured look of fine marble. Along with his FAL and 3 clips, he shouldered a canvas rice sack. A transistor radio bulged in the pocket of his blue shirt. He wore jeans and a faded green baseball cap with the initials CR. The squad leader motioned for him to be still while he listened for the sound of the airplane through the canopy of tall trees and branches that speckled the creek bed with filtered light. When the squad leader was satisfied that the plane was no longer nearby and had not spotted them, he squatted near the creek and, scooping up water with his cupped hand, rinsed his forehead. The new recruit stretched himself over the shallow creek and drank greedily from the cool water.

"Don't drink too much," the squad leader said. "It's a ways to go yet and we have to move fast."

"It's all right," the other replied. "It won't bother me." He stuck his mouth in the water again and with loud slurps took his fill. Then he splashed water on his face to refresh himself.

The squad leader crossed the thin creek, carefully stepping on rocks, leaving no muddy footprints in his wake. He cradled the FAL in his left arm and with his right hand swatted the purple mosquitos that pricked his shoulders and face. His eyes, 2 dark slits, inspected the trees along the creek bed for signs of movement; his habit of eyeing the terrain was an old one and had helped him survive this far. It was so still and quiet here in the shade, away from the trenches and the fighting; even the sky that he could see through the branches was blue and peaceful. They had left Peñas Blancas on foot, following the Pan American Highway till the buzzing of the observation plane made them halt. The squad leader was in a hurry to make the next 4 kilometers and deliver a message to the coman-dante in the farmhouse along the Río Ostallo. He'd be there quicker without this recruit. But that was part of the order—to present the new compa to the comandante and integrate him into the column.

There wasn't much the squad leader liked about the new man. He was a chele who had come in from Costa Rica and had started boasting as soon as he arrived in camp. A man who bragged of his courage was usually a coward, but the squad leader let him go on talking, even as they marched, till the sound of the airplane made them leave the highway. Even the man's pseudonym was terrible— El Chivo. Going to war and he calls himself "the Goat." That rubbed the squad leader the wrong way. And worse, the man didn't listen at all. It might be too late when he learned that lesson.

The squad leader stood in the spotted light filtered by the overhanging branches, his dark Indian eyes on the other man, who had pulled out a plastic canteen from his burlap sack and was now filling it in the creek. It was true that Chivo was strong looking, and maybe he did know about rifles and shooting like he said in camp. Maybe he'd be all right and not like those that get sick with the first mosquito bite and are not good for anything afterwards and you have to send them back. Maybe he would turn out right, the squad leader thought.

Then the squad leader noticed a piece of burnt, camouflaged uniform like the kind the guardia used. It was half buried in the bottom of the creek bed a few meters from where he was standing. He instinctively slipped the FAL into his hands and flipped the safety off. Cautiously, he went to inspect the tunnel where the creek crossed under the highway and water purled in small pools. In the cool shade of the tunnel his ears picked up the buzzing of flies and the rotting smell hit him. In the dim light he found a dead guardia sitting against the wooden pilings with sluggish water up to his waist. A swarm of flies covered the guardia's mouth; the skin had yellowed and stretched tight over the cheekbones and jaw, the eye sockets were caved in. The tropic heat had split open the dead man's stomach, releasing a noxious gas.

The squad leader stepped out from under the small, dark tunnel. Now he knew which creek this was, and what he could find 100 meters farther up. The night they attacked Peñas Blancas, the guardia had fled in disarray and some of Jacinto's men ambushed them while they were crossing this creek; the water had flowed red for days. There must be at least a dozen corpses upstream feeding the vultures, thought the squad leader, and he turned his gaze to Chivo twisting the cap on his plastic canteen.

The squad leader pointed to the tunnel where the creek crossed under the highway till Chivo came over and peeked into the shadows and saw the decomposing body half hidden in the weeds.

A look of disdain crossed the squad leader's face when he saw Chivo go grey and then turn a light shade of green. Chivo's the kind who'll get yellow on us, he thought.

"Come on," the squad leader snapped. "We don't have time to sightsee." The squad leader scrambled up the embankment, through the thick bramble, and not till he reached the clearing of the Pan American Highway did he hear the bush start rustling below, which meant Chivo was following.

The squad leader swept his eyes down the empty tree-lined highway, along the treetops, and across the clear blue sky. Then he slung his FAL over his right shoulder, adjusted the heavy pack high on his back, hand signaled Chivo to stay low, and without delaying any longer, made fast tracks toward Sapoá and the farmhouse on the other side of the Río Ostallo.

Miguel the Campesino

"One of our squads was probing the guardia line near the lime-stone quarry, La Calera. I was number 6, so I was marching near the middle. We hadn't been gone an hour when the strap on my FAL broke, so I carried it gripped by the handle that folds out above the stock. There was no moon or starlight to guide by, and I don't know, but maybe we got lost. We were on a narrow trail with branches scratching our faces and the bush thick all around. The next thing I know the night just exploded in front of us in a flash of fire. The guardia hit us point-blank, cutting down the front of the squad in the first burst. I took 2 hits, here in the hand knocking my rifle out, and through here, in the front and out the back. I went down face first and could hear the compas behind me returning fire as the guardia shouted curses at us.

"The bullets flew for a minute or 2, then both sides ceased firing. My face was half buried in mud and I could tell I was hit bad. The guardia was so close I could hear them in the bush congratulating each other. I decided to play dead and wait for a chance to get out. Then the compas who had taken cover started cursing the guardia with ¡hijo-'e-putas! ¡asesinos! and yelling ¡vivas! to the frente. I knew they were waiting to see if any compas that had been hit could get out, but I couldn't move 'cause the guardia was right next to me. After an eternity I could hear movement in the direction we came from. The compas were pulling back; they figured no one was alive. Soon after, I hear the guardia coming out of the bush, laughing as they looted the compas' bodies. A pistol went off and I almost bolted. One of them very distinctly says, 'We're going to put a bullet in every one of these sons-of-whores.'

"But I didn't move an inch from the way I landed after being hit, and my right hand, you see, had come down like this, as if making the sign of the cross. And I stayed like that, barely breathing. Then a guardia says, 'Look at this son-of-a-whore, he looks like he's making the sign of the cross,' and he kneels down next to me and jerks my wristwatch off, and when he drops my hand, I leave it the same, still making the sign of the cross. Another guardia says, 'Put a bullet in him.' And the one who took the watch, 'cause I recognized the voice, says, 'Ya está muerto.'

"After another eternity, the guardia leaves and I still stay there not moving. I wait forever before opening an eye and see it's still night. I figure I've got to crawl out before daybreak, so ever so slowly I begin to inch my way back, and I crawl about half a kilometer on my belly, hurting badly. I passed out several times—I don't know— but finally the sun comes up over a line of trees and I figure it's safe enough to stand, so I get up and struggle along the trail till I meet a group of our compas who take me to Sapoá where a young Mexican doctor took care of me. After that, they shipped me to Peñas Blancas then here to the hospitalito; I've been here 2 weeks. It's like I asked the Mexican doctor the other day, you think I'll be ready to go back to the front soon?"

Southern Skies

A tense quiet settled over Peñas Blancas as the helicopter high overhead withdrew from sight. Ulises was shoulder-deep in a trench at the outskirts of town with a Belgian FAL strung across his chest, several weeks of beard shagging his face, his eyes stinging irritably from many nights without sleep. He had a clear view of the land sloping toward the marshes, the creek, and the tree line that hung like a background curtain for the 12.7 tripod-mounted Soviet machine gun nest. The 3 compas with the long-barreled machine gun searched the cloudless blue sky for the helicopter's dragonfly silhouette. Ulises killed time, awaiting the results of the helicopter's spotter mission. The tension level in Peñas Blancas went up a couple of notches. It wasn't a long wait. In a few minutes a distinct black, double-tailed push-pull appeared in the sky. The twin-engine aircraft went into a strafing run, its machine guns rattling, aiming for the machine gun nest. The 12.7, hidden behind a wall of sandbags, returned fire. *Tratátátátátátá*, little puffs of grey smoke rose from the 12.7 as the 3 compas moved fast, trying to follow the dive of the fighter plane. The push-pull veered up sharply and came back for another pass. The second time around it came in at a steep 45 degrees, wing-mounted machine guns spitting fire. That's what the Stukas must've looked like, Ulises thought.

The compas with the 12.7 machine gun opened up a rapid fire, the barrel smoking, while the earth jumped up around them. From the opposite side of Peñas Blancas, the .50 caliber joined in, but too far away to be effective. After this run the push-pull went off in the direction of the lake. That's what the helicopter was doing, Ulises figured, giving the position of the 12.7. The compas in the machine gun nest began repairing their sandbags. The tension eased ever so slightly.

Ulises glanced at his watch. 1010 hours. The zigzag of trenches surrounded a bombed-out ranch house with a corral and a barn; next to the ranch house leaned a wooden shack. The morning was bright and fresh after a night of rain, and the upturned earth from the trenches looked fertile and rich to Ulises as he crossed the front length of the ranch house, passed a narrow alley with duckboards over the mud, and stepped into the second low-roofed building he came to. Once an office of some sort, their platoon had cleaned it out and now used it for sleeping quarters where they tried to catch fleeting naps on empty burlap sacks spread over the brick floor. Military gear was stacked in piles around the room, several FALs were propped against a wall, a half-full crate of 7.62 cartridges squatted near a corner. The Popular Sandinista Insurrection Will Triumph was painted in black on one wall. Beneath this was painted,

VIVA EL FSLN
P.L.O.M.

Their main hope for hot coffee was hidden behind a plywood partition in the back of the room where Dany, a Tico, had volunteered to fix a small gas stove. Guto, the tall, wiry Tico with bushy beard and long hippy-type hair, who in the constant shuffling had replaced Gaspar and was head of the platoon, roughly woke up 4 compas who'd been sleeping on the floor. Guto seldom slept, and his red puffy eyes glared at Ulises.

"Anything to eat?" Ulises asked.

"No!" shouted Guto.

"I'm going to sack out a few hours," said Ulises, walking out, leaving Guto to gather the men and their arms and take them out to change the guard. Gaspar had definitely been a better element.

Outside, the morning sun was already high and the day was turning hot and humid. Ulises kept under the roofed walkway, past the empty, humble offices and the one residence long-deserted, with books still scattered on the floor. The restaurant was also abandoned, without chairs or tables. Next to the restaurant was a transport office that had been converted into a mess hall for the General Staff. Next to the mess hall was a modern—now gutted—duty-free store that had belonged to the dictator, where expensive perfumes and liquor had been displayed. The Pan American Highway divided this part of town from the looted and burned Guardia Nacional barracks and the bombed-out immigration building that were across the 2-lane highway. There wasn't one civilian left in Peñas Blancas; the war had driven them away long ago. Only the compas in their military uniforms, with red and black scarves and berets, toting different makes of arms, were in town.

Ulises stepped into the dim light of the mess hall. The skinny black Panamanian who ran the kitchen was sitting down at a table sipping coffee. Indian Joe wore a white T-shirt and blue jeans; a dark blue beanie with a white feather sticking out of it was propped on his head. Most of his front teeth were missing.

"Indian Joe, anything to eat?"

"No, loco, sólo café, just coffee. Best coffee; Indian Joe make some for you."

"No, don't bother. Coffee I don't need."

Ulises felt uptight from lack of sleep and hunger.

"I'll come back later, Joe."

"Sure, anything you say. Joe have steak and potatoes, big salad, sweet cake and rum. Maybe some dancing girls, huh?" Joe liked talking in a mixture of Spanish and pidgin English that usually made Ulises laugh. This time he muttered, "Shit!" as he left the mess hall.

A yellow diesel generator on wheels hummed monotonously nearby as it fed power to the command post under the basement of the former duty-free store. Malek, the Arab-Nica student from Blue-fields, was on duty in the small parking lot in front of the store. He was stripped to his waist and was breaking the concrete near the edge of the parking lot with a pick. Sweat dripped down his face.

"What're you doing, Malek?" Ulises asked.

"The aviation's been hitting us so much, I'm going to dig a trench right here, so I can do duty with peace of mind."

"If you say so," replied Ulises.

The duty-free store was the end of the block. Beyond was the .50-caliber, an open field with knee-high grass waving in the breeze, and further on a grove of guanacaste trees and the Costa Rican border. A balcony on the south side of the duty-free store faced Costa Rica. Beneath that was a basement with part of the wall knocked out for easier access, and sandbags piled inside and outside its walls. That was where the General Staff command post for the Southern Front was located.

Charley was on duty on the balcony, squatting on his haunches, his back against the wall and his FAL resting nearby. Ulises was furious.

"Stand up, Charley!"

"What? What do you mean?"

"I said stand up, damn it. You're on duty, right?"

"But there's no one around."

"Get up and act like a soldier. Is that how you do duty, sitting on your ass?"

Charley stirred; his black puppy eyes looked up at Ulises.

"I'm getting up." He rose and picked up the rifle.

"Don't ever let me see you like that again, or I'll break you in two. Understand?"

Charley nodded. Ulises stepped down the muddy, slippery sandbags to the basement and greeted the compa on sentry duty. There was an earthy coolness inside the command post. Two women radio operators were the only ones in there, besides the sentry. One of them was fiddling with the dial on the big shortwave radio, adjusting her earphones and testing the hand-held mike. She was big and heavy, with dark sweat stains under her armpits, her hair cut short and a thin wispy mustache running across her top lip. She never gave Ulises information, so he didn't bother asking her if there was any news. The other operator Ulises had never seen before. She was a golden brown color, with curly hair and green eyes. It looked like the big one was breaking her in.

There was no one from the General Staff around, not Jacinto, Marvin, or Wachan. Ulises went back out and climbed the sandbag steps up to the balcony.

Charley was looking more alive, and Ulises acknowledged him. In the parking lot Malek had broken through the concrete and was now shoveling spadefuls of earth, the sweat running down his back. A white jeep with green and brown paint splotches and all the windows and mirrors smashed out of it so they wouldn't reflect the sun came roaring down the road from Sapoá and braked to a screeching halt in the parking lot. The driver, a well-built chele with shoulder-length blond hair, in a tight-fitting olive green T-shirt and camouflaged pants, jumped out. A .45 automatic was strapped to his waist. Tigre was the best of the drivers in the mobile unit who did the 6 km from Sapoá to Peñas Blancas at breakneck speed so the aviation wouldn't catch them on the open road. Tigre had the air of Errol Flynn in *Captain Blood.*

"¿Yhay, Tigre?" Ulises greeted him.

"Have you seen Wachan?" replied Tigre, adjusting his green beret.

"Not today. I just came from the command post. There's no one there."

"¡Mierda! That means I'm going to have to drive back to Sapoá. Damn, there's more aviation out today than buzzards." Tigre stomped his big boots in the shade of the corridor and wiped his brow with the palm of his hand.

"Anything in there?" he asked, motioning to the mess hall.

"Gotta ask Indian Joe," answered Ulises.

"Let me see if I can get a bite before going back."

"Sure. I'll see you later," Ulises said and continued down the corridor, heading for the little shack next to the farmhouse.

Along the chain link fence that separated the block of buildings from the Pan American Highway, a papaya tree was growing large green and yellow fruit. It will be ripe in a few more days, Ulises thought as he reached the other end of the block. He went past the platoon's quarters, across the narrow alley with the duckboards over the mud, and passed in front of the abandoned ranch house and the zigzag of trenches, then rounded the corner of the ranch house and slipped into the dusty, unpainted wooden shack. Sunlight filtered in through the warped planks, but it was dry and he wanted very badly to sleep. Ulises leaned the FAL against a wall of the shack, butt on the ground. He threw his web belt with the 3 clips next to it, unbuttoned his shirt and untied the laces on his Georgia boots. He was ready to sit on a wooden pallet when his eyes caught the crescent shape of the scorpion stinger.

"¡Hijo 'e puta!" Ulises pulled back in surprise, then got up close to get a better look. The scorpion was the size of his little finger and the color of cooked shrimp.

"Another second and I'd have sat on you," Ulises said, not quite sure what to do with it. He could smash it, but that seemed like overkill. He looked around for something to trap it with. He found an empty olive jar with the label still on it. Using a twig, Ulises forced the scorpion into the jar, then turned it upside down on the ground so the scorpion could be seen but could not get out.

"There you go, little guy; I'll let you out later if you renounce your somocista tendencies."

Ulises folded his shirt for a pillow and stretched out on the hard pallet, his boots still on, beret over his face. In a minute he heard the jeep go tearing up the road. In a few more seconds he was snoring. He dreamt the weird dream of the guardia charging at him, their faces yellow and distorted. Always at this point in the dream his rifle jammed and he got that strange dream panic and a loud TRATÁTÁTÁTÁTÁTÁ going off in his ear, which startled him awake to find the whole shack shaking like a leaf.

Ulises rolled off the pallet, and with the same motion grabbed his FAL, knocking over the jar and freeing the scorpion. He couldn't be bothered with that now. Shirtless and in a low crouch, a tight grip on the FAL, he ran out of the shack into the bright day sun. Pedro and Carlos, who had been billeted in back of the farmhouse, came running, all excited. Pedro was shouting and pointing to the sky.

"Damn! That buzzard almost took us all!"

"It was the supersonic," added Carlos, his eyes big behind the horn-rimmed glasses. "Just dropped out of the sky. Couldn't hear him, just came in blasting."

"He'll probably do another run," said Pedro.

"Right," responded Ulises. "Make sure everyone's covered on your side. I'll pass the word over here to stay in the trenches." Ulises ran over to the command post where Guto, Dany, and the other compas were still spread out flat on the floor waiting for the next strafing.

"How's everyone?" Ulises asked.

"I busted my elbow jumping for cover," cursed Guto, clutching his left elbow.

"I'm going to hit some trenches," Dany said, rushing outside past Ulises.

"I'll wait it out in here," Guto said. The other compas who'd been sleeping at the time of the attack agreed with Guto. Ulises dashed back out and took cover in the zigzag trenches that ran in front of the farmhouse. Cleto, Fredy, and Chele were already in there, waiting for the return of the A-37.

Twenty minutes searching the sky and nothing appeared. After another 10 minutes, the all clear passed from mouth to mouth. Everyone cautiously left their positions in the trenches. Ulises sat on a crate under the porch of the ranch house cleaning the mud from the barrel and stock of his FAL. Guto came over with Dany and sat on a bench next to Ulises.

"I don't understand the General Staff," Guto said, in a low mood. "They want us to do more duty than we have men for. Some of the men haven't had a decent sleep in a week. They're falling asleep on duty. ¡Mierda!"

"Maybe we can put Joaquín and Cleto on duty. They seem like they can take an extra turn without complaining. I'll have to explain it to them."

"You just order them to do it," responded Guto.

"It helps if they know why they're doing extra duty."

Guto mused that over. Ulises continued cleaning his FAL. Cleto was in the trench in front of him trying to sleep, and Dany sat silently next to Guto. Then the pounding rattle of machine guns caught them without warning. Guto and Dany dived for the alleyway and Ulises threw himself down inside the ranch house. Bullets splattered the wall they'd been sitting against, and bits of brick and dust jumped off and landed on them as the *varoom* of the jet racking them with Gatling guns zoomed overhead. Everyone remained with their faces to the ground. Ulises hugged the earth tighter than he'd ever done a woman. The jet came roaring back for another run. He's pinpointed us, thought Ulises.

The A-37 came in shooting rockets. The papaya tree by the chain link fence exploded in a cloud of dust. Another rocket hit near the corral, shaking dirt loose from the old roof of the ranch house.

After the rocket attack, the A-37 flew off in the direction of Sapoá. Everyone scrambled up and inspected the damage. The brick wall where Ulises, Guto, and Dany had been sitting sported a dozen holes that left the bricks all chewed up.

"¡A la gran pu . . . !" Ulises exclaimed, examining the holes.

"Close. Very close," agreed Guto.

"Look," said Dany, picking up something from the ground. It was the projectile of the Gatling the A-37 was firing. Dany dropped it in Ulises's open palm. It was bronze-colored, about 3 inches long, and twice as thick as a pencil. It was still warm.

"One of these could tear you up pretty bad," Ulises commented, handing it back to Dany. Dany weighed the lead in his hand, then closed his fingers over it and put it in his pocket.

Cleto, Fredy, and Chele stood around with them, talking excitedly for several minutes. When the mood calmed, those who were on duty returned to their posts. Dany and Guto disappeared inside the platoon's quarters, and Ulises went back to his spot in front of the ranch house and continued cleaning his FAL. Dany, the cook, came looking for him in a few minutes.

"Ulises, I've got some good news," Dany said.

"What is it?"

"I just got word from the quartermaster that some supplies came in. They want us to send some men for it."

"Some men? Hmm. Where's Guto?"

"He just fell asleep, right now."

Ulises thought this over for a minute.

"Everyone else is on duty, so it's going to have to be you and me, Dany." Ulises hadn't slept in 24 hours, except for the brief nap interrupted by the jet. Guto hadn't slept in at least 2 days.

Ulises shouldered his FAL and went off with Dany in the direction of the border. Instead of going along the walkway of Peñas Blancas, they crossed over to the other side of the chain link fence that ran along the Pan American and walked along the edge of the asphalt highway. As they passed the duty-free store, they noticed that Malek had finished digging his trench and was now visible only from his chest up.

They walked south toward the border. El Gordo, with his curly hair bleached by the sun and his thick brown biceps in a sleeveless T-shirt, was manning the .50, its barrel pointing to the sky and surrounded by sandbags. To their left was the radio hut, with the tall antenna and the flagpole flying the red and black flag. Next to the radio hut came the garage where they had the mobile units, including the armored vehicles they had improvised for the assault on Peñas Blancas. The vehicles were regular motorcars with thick armor plating welded onto the outside; slits were cut into the plating where a compa could stick a gun through to fire. There were 3 of these vehicles parked there.

They crossed the checkpoint that was the border, with armed compas hanging around the long upright, unused needle. Beyond was Costa Rica, but the Costa Ricans had withdrawn everything 5 km because of the war, so this strip was really no-man's-land. The Front had some medical units and the quartermaster stationed where the Tico aduana used to be under a grove of guanacaste trees.

Dany puffed a cigarette as they strolled along next to the thin trees that straddled the highway, the gravel making a crunching sound under their boots. Dany was a short, tough man. He had raised himself in the streets of San José, Costa Rica, and had learned to use a 12-inch blade to carve anything and anyone in his way. At 32, he was the oldest member of the platoon, but his face looked more like 45 and mistreated. He was a member of a political party in Costa Rica and had come into the front with Guto. They were kind of like Mutt and Jeff. Every now and then as they walked along the side of the road in the warm sun, Dany would break out in a gravel-voiced rendition of an old cabaret song, "Todos dicen que soy, el muñeco de la ciudad."

It was about a kilometer from the border to where the big semi-trailer was parked under a canopy of trees. When they were still several hundred meters away, they heard compas shouting, "¡Aviación, aviación!" Ulises and Dany broke into a trot, heading for the supply station. Everyone was running for cover. One of the compas was shouting, "¡Línea vietnamita, compitas, línea vietnamita!"

Ulises could hear the roar of the engines above the trees, then through a clearing in the branches he saw the big-bellied 2-engine prop AC-47 gunship, coming in low over the treetops, .50-caliber machine guns firing from its port sides. In comparison to the stinging, quick action of the push-pulls and A-37s, this was a slow, lumbering elephant. Ulises formed part of the line and along with the other compas opened up with his FAL, trying to lead the plane

before squeezing off a few rounds, aiming for the propeller. *Kapow!*
Kapow! Kapow! Little puffs of smoke rose up between the trees. The
AC-47 made one slow pass and left.

The compas returned to what they'd been doing before the
gunship appeared. The semitrailer was parked next to the Tico
aduana, well hidden by the trees. Small offices across from the
aduana had been turned into medical units. Dany checked in with
Félix, the quartermaster. Ulises waited in the dappled light of the
shade, talking with compas, trying to ignore his fatigue and hunger.
Dany returned with a big grin on his beat-up face. He'd gotten their
rations plus a little extra, a dozen cans of peanuts and a little gas
cylinder to hook up to their stove. Dany was very happy.

Ulises and Dany split the 100 cans of tuna and the 50 smaller
cans of condensed milk into 2 large green plastic bags and headed
back to Peñas Blancas. Ulises carried the dozen cans of peanuts in
his bag while Dany toted the gas cylinder. Before leaving the cover
of trees they shared a can of peanuts, then started out along the side
of the road under the hot afternoon sun. These rations had to last 20
compas at least 5, maybe 6 days. He'd let Guto and Dany do the
distribution, though it was very simple: 1 can of tuna and 1 of those
demitasse cans of condensed milk per compa per day. The cans of
peanuts would be split amongst them all. Simple arithmetic; his
ration should last him easy. He couldn't look at canned tuna anymore; the oily smell made him queasy. Yesterday he'd given most of
his tuna to Fredy, who'd been complaining. Last week he and Cleto
had come upon a cow carcass split open—by a rustler, most likely.
They didn't hesitate to shoo away the flies and cut what meat they
could from the bones and give it to Dany to salt and boil. Ulises had
heard stories of columns that had survived weeks on green mangos or
who took to shooting monkeys out of trees for their meals. He
finally willed himself to ignore hunger when Indian Joe shot a
buzzard down from the sky, plucked it, boiled it and offered it to the
platoon. No one but the cook would touch it, and he licked his
fingers. Ulises thought of that and of his first day in Nicaragua when
they entered camp and were offered tortillas, canned tuna, and 2-
ounce cans of sweet lactose; he'd even soaked up the oil in the
bottom of the can. Now the tuna was driving him fishy, and it was as

if the dead fish were taking their revenge on him because they were a necessity. He kept switching the cumbersome bag and the FAL from shoulder to shoulder so his back wouldn't stiffen up; a trickle of sweat started down the side of his face. He thought what a shitty thing war was; literally wiping your ass with grass stuff. It's you trying to kill someone you don't even know, and someone who doesn't know you or give a damn about it trying to kill you without even asking your name, or what you've done, or if you're any good with the ladies. In this type of small war, killing was very personal because the combatants were so few; the Nicas usually counted a relative on the other side, and as an internationalist, you could be close enough in combat to see the face of the enemy. See what he looked like before you squeezed the trigger. There was nothing he could do about it except, if and when the time came, do it as well as he could. He didn't realize it, but Dany had fallen several meters behind by the time he reached the upright needle and Gordo with the .50.

Malek came rushing out of his trench in the duty-free store parking lot when he saw Ulises.

"Ulises! They got Tigre!"

"What? When? Are you sure?" Ulises put the green plastic bag down.

"They're bringing him in right now."

Ulises was stunned. "What happened?"

"The jet caught him on his way back to Sapoá. Guto wants to see you right away. He said he'd be at the ranch house."

"Damn," Ulises said, "damn." He looked at Malek and lifted the green bag onto his shoulder.

"I'm going to see Guto," he said.

The load of canned food seemed much heavier as he carried it the last 100 meters. Ulises noticed that the papaya tree that had seemed almost ready to ripen its fruit was now just a splintered trunk. He left the bag in the platoon's quarters and went in search of Guto. The platoon leader was sitting by himself in front of the ranch house, in the same spot where the jet had earlier left the bullet-pocked brick wall.

Guto's shoulders were hunched over, his elbows on his knees, his long face in his hands. On one side his FAL leaned against the wall. Guto's eyes were very red. He looked drawn and haggard; deep creases etched his forehead. He glanced up at Ulises.

"Have you heard about Tigre?"

"Malek just told me."

"I'm very depressed about it."

"So am I," said Ulises, sitting down on the bench next to Guto.

Guto sat up. "That's not all, we're also having problems with Charley."

"What do you mean?"

"He wants to be sent out. Says he can't take it anymore. He's too scared. I want you to talk to him, see if you can calm him down."

"Where is he?"

"He's with Pedro and Carlos; they're talking to him, but he refuses to carry his rifle or anything."

"I'll go see him right now."

"One more thing, Ulises. The men who were sleeping I sent over as an honor guard for Tigre. They're having a wake for him right now over by the warehouse."

Ulises felt a heavy weariness. "I'll drop by after I talk with Charley."

Ulises stepped around Guto, turned left at the corner of the ranch house, went past the unpainted shack where he'd been strafed that morning, and continued down to the back of the ranch house with its small corral and barn. Pedro and Carlos were billeted here and had made themselves comfortable, bringing in a table and stringing up a hammock. They slept inside the barn on piles of newspapers and hay. Charley, who'd been sitting down inside the barn, came running up to Ulises, his eyes a little wild. He carried no rifle or clips.

"What's the matter, Charley?"

"I don't know. I'm scared, Ulises. I'm scared of the plane." His tone was pathetic, that of a whimpering child.

"I know you're scared, Charley; we're all scared. But you have to hold onto your balls like everyone else."

"I can't, Ulises; I'm scared the plane is going to kill me."

"What are you talking about? There's no planes right now."

"But it's going to come back, Ulises, you know it's going to come back. And it's going to kill me. I know it, it's going to kill me."

"Grab a hold of yourself, man. You see anyone else acting like you? We've all been under fire, but nobody's running. What if we all did what you want to do? What if we all got up and left 'cause we were scared? Then what?"

"I can't help it. I'm scared and I want to get out. Please Ulises, send me to Costa Rica!"

"Wait a minute, Charley . . ." Ulises grabbed him by the shoulders, the anger starting to rise.

"No, no, I want to get out, I want to get out . . ."

Charley's voice cracked and he trembled like a leaf; Ulises could see there was nothing to be done with him.

"All right, calm down, I'll tell Guto to send you out. Get your personal gear together and wait here for Guto."

"Thank you, Ulises." Charley with his puppy dog eyes scampered back into the barn.

Ulises, disgusted, went to find Guto. He was at platoon quarters.

"He's out of it, Guto; I don't think there's anything we can do for him. He seems to be shell-shocked."

"I tried talking to him, but he wouldn't listen. If we send him out, we're going to be short a man. We're already overextended."

"What can we do? Charley is worthless now."

Guto stroked his beard. "Scared shitless of the aviation is what he is."

"You gonna take him across the border?"

"I guess so. We have medical units over there, right?"

"Correct."

"I better take him over there now, I guess . . ."

Guto left to get Charley. Ulises stood outside the door and smoked a cigarette he had pulled out of a plastic Baggie in his pocket. He took the last drag on the cigarette, crushing the butt on the walkway planks with his boot and exhaling the smoke into the late afternoon air.

The sun's shadow was slanting across the tall, peaked face of the immigration building as Ulises crossed the Pan American Highway with a heavy heart. Next to the immigration building a cavernous abandoned warehouse sheltered a group of compas gathered around a wooden box. Ulises silently joined the group. The coffin was made of 2 empty FAL crates nailed together. Ulises, his head bowed, stood before the body of Tigre. One of the compas lifted the green plastic sheet for a last look at his comrade. Tigre's body was revealed in the dim, hazy light of the warehouse. It was not the Tigre Ulises had talked with today; that Tigre was alive and handsome. This one was dead, torn nearly in half from his chest to his groin, his nose smashed and his face broken from the crash, his thick blond hair matted with blood.

They covered Tigre again with the green plastic sheet. Ulises turned and left the honor guard formed in 2 lines on either side of the coffin. Sometime today or tonight they would offer him a final salute before burial. Ulises headed back to platoon quarters, emotionally and physically drained.

Crossing the highway again, he suddenly felt bitter at all the pseudo-theorists sitting around in comfortable cafés, criticizing the strategy of insurrection in their smooth university tone, all the while keeping their hands clean so that after the triumph they could march in with their cameras and tape recorders and make video specials on the revolution; heroic actions that would surely make them even more famous as theorists, or whatever shit. He was no military hero by any means, but he'd done every task well. He had nothing to be ashamed of. Like Kike had said to him once, "for the cafetín revolutionaries, I wish them one minute of war—just one."

Guto was already back at platoon quarters when Ulises arrived.

"What happened with Charley?"

"I took him over to the medics, but there's no out passes for 24 hours. The General Staff has sent word to prepare for a guardia attack tonight. They've breached our line a few kilometers from here, so I couldn't get Charley out."

"So where is he?"

"It would almost be funny if it wasn't pathetic. I had the medics give him something to calm him down, so in the middle of the injection, some planes came overhead strafing and dropping a few bombs. Should've seen Charley; he beat all of us under the beds. Poor guy made us all laugh. He's calm now, sleeping like a baby in the barn. Medics say when the injection wears off tomorrow, to bring him back."

"All right, now what?"

"We're short a man and we have to post everyone tonight. Those are orders."

"Even the compas who haven't slept in 24 hours?"

"Even those poor bastards. They'll have to make it through another night."

"I better get started on it, then. I'll take some of the guys out by the creek to relieve the other squad."

"Ulises, one more thing. The General Staff wants us to pick 4 or 5 of our best men to send to Sapoá tonight. I think they need some reinforcements over there. Do you want to take them?"

"I guess so. I can take Quincho, Joaquín, Ernesto, Fredy maybe, and myself. Any idea what it's about?"

"No, but I'll tell the General Staff we'll have the men ready. I think they're going to move you out after nightfall. You better get some rest. I'm going back to the General Staff and see if we can't get some replacements. Good luck, Ulises."

Guto stepped out into the corridors of the bombed-out town and went off in the direction of the General Staff command post. Ulises slung his FAL over one shoulder and went out to the ranch house and the zigzag of trenches, heading for the shack where he kept his gear.

The sun was setting behind the distant hills, leaving bright red and orange streaks in its wake. Ulises stood for a moment gazing at the splendid sunset, forgetting his hunger and his fatigue, saving himself for the night ahead. He saw Tigre's face before him and the anger rose and gathered in watery pools in his eyes. A glittering light appeared on the horizon, slowly approaching Peñas Blancas. A deep, sad sigh shook Ulises as he gazed at the light, thinking it was the first star of the night, then he realized it was not a star at all, but a helicopter, probably the same one that had appeared that morning. It was coming from a northerly direction, from Sapoá, as did all the aviation. It was surely spotting coordinates for the guardia artillery. It would be pinpointing their positions for the barrage that would follow, perhaps the prelude to the guardia counterattack on

Peñas Blancas. It was the guardia helicopter—he was sure of it now. Already he could hear the distant rumbling of the guardia artillery firing and see the faraway flash explosions hitting along the ridge at La Calera and advancing toward Sapoá.

Combat in the Ravine

Ulises, along with 4 compas from his platoon, boarded a jeep and headed out of Peñas Blancas under the cover of night. He sat next to the driver, watching the shadows of the countryside go by. A half-moon cast black silhouettes of trees and outlined the soft rolling hills in the distance. Before the blown-up bridge of the Río Pita, Ulises saw the shadowy form of the farmhouse where weeks ago he'd gone to get the FALs for his squad. The FAL named Miriam rubbed the inside of his leg, 3 loaded clips were wrapped around his waist, and the cool night breeze caressed his face. He was dead tired, and the anticipation of the coming hours left him alternately calm, then jittery.

Big-bellied Joaquín, sitting in back of the jeep with Eddy, Quincho, and the Colombian Chele, wondered why they were being jeeped out of Peñas Blancas and feared they were on their way to assault Hill 50, where the guardia was entrenched with several .50-caliber machine guns. He drummed his fat fingers along the wooden stock of his FAL and wished for the ride to last a long time. Eddy sat next to Joaquín, not caring where he was going, and dozing off every so often only to be jarred awake by the jeep's bumpy ride. Quincho sat behind Ulises, the wind blowing through his hair, glad to be out of Peñas Blancas and hoping for a mission where he might see action. After all, Quincho thought to himself, he hadn't joined up to do guard duty, he'd come to fight, and up to now, he hadn't once fired his rifle at the enemy. Chele hummed a cumbia in his head to keep the fear out and watched the passing hills and shadowy trees as the jeep sped its way along the moonlit highway.

The ride lasted 15 minutes.

"We're in Sapoá," revealed the driver, stopping the jeep abruptly under a large tree in the plaza of a small, bombed-out, deserted town totally in ruins. They got out of the jeep and were presented by the driver to a tall, broad-shouldered compa with shoulder-length hair and a black beret. Comandante Julio was his name and he was in command of a group of compas who waited in the night shadows of the plaza. Ulises gave him the names of the compas from Peñas and was told to take as much ammo as they could carry from several crates of 7.62s that were stacked nearby. Ulises and the other compas silently stuffed their pockets with the long, thin cartridges.

Comandante Julio formed all the compas in the plaza into a column of 3 squads. There was much shuffling and clanking of gear as the compas got into a single file, then the comandante lifted a Browning Automatic Rifle over one shoulder and gave the order for the march to begin. The column headed off on a rough gravel road pitted with holes, and the compas stumbled along, their gear bouncing noisily up and down, till after a while the noise became the steady rhythm of the march. The half-moon was partially rubbed out by clouds, but the rest of the sky was covered with stars, illuminating the bleak countryside. Comandante Julio towered above the middle of the column; Ulises and the compas from Peñas Blancas integrated the rear guard. Ulises searched for constellations in the vibrant heavens and found Orion; the column seemed to be marching in a northwest direction.

The dirt country road went up a small ridge, then down into a narrow, dark valley where mist hugged the ground and the hills rose up sharply. In the heart of this valley the column was halted by sentries next to the tall, black tower of the limestone quarry known as La Calera. Ulises could hear whispering going on all along the column. Comandante Julio left his position to investigate the situation in front. Quincho asked, "Why are we stopping?"

"I don't know," answered Ulises. On the opposite side of the hills, the guardia began a mortar barrage with the hollow sounding *whoosh* of their 81mm. Everyone listened for the sound of the incoming. Several white phosphorus explosions landed along the hills 300 meters away and all the compas squatted low, waiting to see which way the barrage was moving. The guardia mortars kept firing, the dull echo reverberating through the valley, the shells landing along the ridgeline, sweeping the distant side of the slopes.

Comandante Julio returned to his place and gave the word to begin the march again. The column continued along the road that was no more than a wide gravelly path leading to the handful of houses that was the settlement at Sotacaballo. More sentries met them and they left half a squad there to reinforce that position. The rest of the column continued marching near the edge of the dirt road now running parallel to the foot of the ridge, then they went off the road, struggling along a dry creek bed hidden under a cover of trees. They stayed on the creek bed till the ridge came together with some foothills, forming a tight, narrow ravine through which the dry creek bed and the road both passed. Once inside the ravine, the starlight was blocked out by the thick foliage, and they had to feel their way along a thin path, bumping into each other and cursing when they knocked their heads on low branches, watching where the shadow in front had been swallowed up by the blackness. Co-mandante Julio told them to shut up, keep their spacing, and make as little noise as possible. Ulises, feeling the effects of sleepless nights and the several kilometers they'd marched, was sweating profusely, and the FAL weighed heavily on his shoulders.

About 0100 hours they made contact with other compas who'd been ensconced in the ravine for the past 12 hours. Comandante Julio held a brief conference with the compa in charge, then gave the instructions: the column was to relieve the compas in the ravine and take over their positions. The setup was an ambush, with the compas spread out in a half-circle, bisected by the same dirt road and dry creek bed they'd been marching on earlier. Comandante Julio stationed himself with the Browning in the dry creek bed next to the dirt road. Ulises and the compas from Peñas Blancas were led by another compa along a trail, hidden in the bush, that ran halfway up the ravine. Every 7 or 8 meters the compa who was leading them would withdraw someone from the darkness and send him scurrying back down the path and place a new compa in the bush. Ulises was placed behind a thick tree and surrounded by knee-high brush. The last thing the compa told Ulises before disappearing into the night was, "I will be a bit to the right of you. Do not leave this position no

matter what happens; this is Patria Libre o Morir, compita, understood?"

Ulises understood. He felt quite alone then, surrounded by the
impenetrable darkness; though he knew Quincho was to the left of
him and the other compa to his right, he guessed this was the flank.
He carefully placed the 3 loaded clips he carried in the soft earth
where he could feel them; he still had plenty of rounds in his pockets
and a loaded clip in the FAL. He peered into the ravine, moving his
sight in circles, trying to catch the features of the terrain in the
corner of his retina instead of looking directly into the blackness.
After a few minutes, he could make out the skeletal forms of tall,
thin trees that filled the cleft of the ravine. He thought how strange
it would be to die here, in total darkness, not even seeing the earth.
His fear of dying twisted around in his heart; he wished he would
never die, but if he had to do it, he could do it now. He resolved in
himself that he would never let them take him alive; the thought of
being in their hands, at their mercy, was like a bath of cold water. If I
die, I go with a battle cry on my lips, "¡Que se rinda tu madre!"

Tic-tic-tic. Aaawrk! Aaawrk! Strange, exotic cacophonies
moved thickly through the bush. A mosquito came buzzing around
his face. ¡Zas! he slapped at it and missed. Seconds later, another
mosquito—or the same one—buzzed his ear. It was a hopeless situation. A thousand mosquitos and gnats owned the night. He pulled
his beret tight down on his head and stroked his thin beard, wondering how long this would last. After a while, he silently shifted his
body to ease the cramp in his muscles and propped the long, heavy
barrel of the FAL on a low-hanging branch, then rested his back
against the soft earth. A hundred unrelated thoughts crossed his
mind: the Miriam he now held in his hands, the other Miriam, his
vida loca, the idea of killing. These thoughts rushed, stumbling
through his brain, with no order or logic whatsoever. He didn't want
to get too comfortable, thinking of the red fire ants that could make
a man howl in agony; he pulled away from the earth, itching (psy-
chologically?) all over under his clothing, and he methodically
scratched his limbs and back in the dark. The insect noise increased
and changed tempo; fireflies appeared and disappeared, unreal like
hyperspace in a sci-fi movie. The tension soon got unbearable, and

he felt like screaming out into the blackness for something to happen, but the next instant he wished for nothing to happen until dawn.

Several hours went by with only the incessant concert whirl of insects and the occasional nocturnal creature that screeched in the bush. Every so often Ulises could hear compas whispering to each other, then the hush that quickly followed. There were strict orders not to make any noise or do anything that might reveal their position. Ulises, burning up energy with the waiting, felt his weariness all the way down the barrel of the FAL. His eyes burned with desire for sleep; his anxiousness turned to a nervous calm. An incredible yearning to doze off hit him, then he remembered stories of how the guardia would sneak up on a compa and cut his throat and the compa wouldn't know it till the last second when it was too late. So Ulises forced himself to stay awake by taking deep breaths, and he continued scanning the inky darkness.

The night cacophonies grew ever more intense till it seemed Ulises would go deaf; then, suddenly, the insects hushed and the ravine became strangely still and quiet. A distant, faint rumbling like a motor running slowly approached the ravine. Ulises sat up, listening to the motor sound getting louder and closer, then idling, then getting louder and closer again. The tension in Ulises's gut made him feel like puking in the stagnant, suffocating heat surrounded by the unfriendly terrain. Dark, indefinable shapes appeared at the threshold of the ravine and halted. Ulises steeled himself and quietly lifted the FAL and pushed it forward a few inches so the muzzle would clear the brush, curled his finger lightly around the trigger, and felt his chest pounding against the wooden stock.

The rumbling sound entered the heart of the ravine just as a grey gloomy dawn peeked over the ridge. Two short-nosed trucks were faintly revealed creeping down the misty dirt road with blackout lights barely glowing; 3 ghostlike guardias walked a few paces ahead of them. They progressed cautiously with the trucks stopping every few feet while the foot guardia figured out which way the road turned, then they would press forward again. Ulises felt the hairs on his neck stand straight and tingle right up under his beret. Moisture formed on his forehead and his palms turned sweaty watching the ghostly guardia convoy seeming to float through the mist. He gasped for breath, but the air was too thin and his diaphragm too tight; in that coil of his stomach, butterflies were hatched.

Then the convoy halted its penetration of the ravine. The trucks were still not in range of the ambush, and the foot guardia seemed to be trying to figure out if they should continue or not. The guardia waited an eternity, engines on low idle as if wanting more light, then with the ravine still in grey darkness, they proceeded as before, crawling slowly over the bumpy, sandy road. Ulises followed the second truck with the muzzle of his FAL as the convoy reached his position; he held his fire, waiting for the signal from the coman-dante, but nothing happened. He could feel his heart pounding against the rifle stock. The convoy was halfway through the ravine, and still the trucks crept forward almost on top of the compas lying in ambush near the road. Then one of the foot guardia stopped and raised his right arm as if he was going to point something out or shout a warning, and at that exact same instant the roar of the Browning blasted him against the hood of the lead truck. In the same volley the truck cab was riddled with deadly fire that smashed the front window; the truck jerked forward and slipped off the edge of the road, crashing into a tree, where it burst into a giant fireball, illuminating the entire ravine. For one split second the scene was frozen in Ulises's eyes like in a flash photo: the lead truck on fire, orange flames mingling with screams as guardias scrambled to jump off, the guardia faces on the other truck peering behind guardrails with a wide-eyed mixture of dread and surprise. The following in-stant the ravine was torn apart by the roaring fusillade of semiauto-matic fire that ripped into the convoy. Muzzle flashes and tracers crisscrossed like crazed fireflies, lighting up the greyness of the morning. Ulises held his breath so his aim would be steady, peered through the v sight, and squeezed off several rounds into the cab of the second truck, shattering the windows and knocking the driver back against the seat. The truck jammed in reverse, jerking back-wards and throwing off some of the guardia, who crashed to the ground with loud curses. The truck made it a few desperate meters before the wheels started spinning in the sandy earth; concentrated fire shattered the rest of the truck cab, and all movement from that truck stopped. The shooting from the compas hidden in the bush looked like yellow flaming tongues darting in and out, with the repetitious roar of the Browning interspersed with the sharp crack of the FALs. The first truck was burning in the center of the ravine, smoking out the guardia who were shouting and cursing and returning fire as best they could from behind the guardrails of the second truck; another group of guardias had taken cover along the depression of the creek bed and from there tried to cover the retreat. Hundreds of tracers flashed through the ravine, zipped by overhanging leaves, and snapped branches. Ulises rolled his back against the tree and quickly changed clips, setting aside the empty one and bringing the loaded ones closer to him. He snapped back the bolt on the FAL and tried to pick his moment, listening to the sound of the fight. The melancholy roar of the Browning swept the road and was punctuated by the ear-splitting KAPOW of the FALs. Concentrated at the opposite end of the ravine was the *ping! ping!* shooting of the Galils and the heavy groan of the Garands. Intermingled with the noise of battle was the guardia's cursing and the thud of bullets slamming into trees. Nearby a compa yelled out, "¡Hijos 'e puta, ríndanse!" And the guardia cursed back amid the pinging sound of bullets hitting the truck where they had taken cover. A guardia in the creek bed shouted, "¡Viva Somoza!" and a compa responded, "¡Viva Monimbó! ¡Viva el Frente Sandinista!"

The pitch of the small arms rose in intensity, and thick clouds of acrid grey gunpowder smoke drifted like fog through the ravine. No one's going to survive this, thought Ulises. The crazy fear made him recklessly brave. He flipped the FAL to automatic, gripping the hand guard tightly and cushioning the butt against his shoulder. He leaped out from behind the tree and released several short, quick bursts into the guardia in the creek bed, kicking up the dirt around them. As he fired each burst, he grunted to himself, "This one's for Rubén Salazar, and for Toño and Ulises Tapia!" then jumped back behind the tree. The barrel of his FAL glowed red-hot, and Ulises could reach out and touch the heat of battle.

A fat guardia sheltered behind the second truck lifted a short, thick-barreled grenade launcher to his shoulder. WHOAMP! The grenade arched through the trees like a dying quail trailing sparks, landed several meters from Ulises, bounced once, rolled a few feet into the brush and exploded in an ear-crunching BOOM! that scattered red-hot, razor-sharp bits of steel and shredded the leaves above Ulises. AAAY! A painful scream came from where the grenade exploded. Ulises sat his ass against the base of the tree, ears ringing, the noise of the fight sounding far away. He tried to change clips, but fumbled the loaded one onto his lap and sat there, unable to do anything. He shook his head, trying to get the stars out, then struggled with the clip. The back-and-forth of the small arms sounded like the roar of the ocean in a seashell, and near where the grenade exploded, a compa was shouting, "I'm hit, I'm hit!"

Ulises finally worked in the clip and slammed the 7.65 into the chamber with a yank of the bolt. The firing now changed tempo and slowed to sporadic bursts before falling off into a strange silence. Ulises's heart still sped along to its own rhythm, his ears felt stuffed with cotton, his mouth was bone dry, and his limbs trembled with excitement and the rush of battle. "Owie!!" he said to himself, leaning the still-hot barrel of the FAL against the tree trunk while he wiped the sweat from his eyes. He couldn't get his legs to stop shaking, so he grabbed them with his hands till they slowed down a bit. Then he became worried about the silence, till the compas burst into cheers of ¡Viva el Frente Sandinista, muera Somoza! He carefully parted some branches and gazed upon the scene. Several dead and wounded guardia were scattered along the dirt road and among the trucks; a thick black column of smoke rose from the truck that had smashed into the tree. One of the wounded guardia started a horrible moaning from somewhere beneath the first truck, then a pause followed by the same voice pleading, "Kill me, for the love of Christ! Kill me!" Ulises couldn't see the guardia, but it seemed like the moaning was coming from the smouldering vehicle. Their orders were to stay hidden in the bush till the comandante gave the all clear.

Near where the grenade had exploded, a low moaning could be heard. When the FAL cooled, Ulises cradled it in his arms and crawled on his elbows and knees, his head throbbing, to where the grass had been blackened by the explosion. Quincho was lying on his back. The fragmentation of the grenade had torn into his right foot, calf, and upper thigh; his pant leg was in shreds and bright red with blood. Quincho, who was spread out on the earth, his FAL nearby, breathing heavily and eyes glassy, smiled wanly when Ulises crawled up to him. "Hijos de la gran . . . They got me, Ulises," Quincho cursed, his eyes dazed and his mouth dry. Ulises looked over the wound, he couldn't tell how much steel Quincho had taken; his foot and the whole length of his leg were a mangled mess of flesh. Ulises took his shirt off and wrapped it snugly around the leg, using the sleeves to tie it with.

"We have to wait for the all clear," he told Quincho, "then we'll see about getting you out. Just relax and rest for now; don't use up your energy talking. I'll stay here with you, so you have nothing to worry about."

Quincho gazed up at Ulises and muttered, "Did we hit them good?"

"Les dimos en la madre," responded Ulises, not knowing how many of their own were down, or whether they'd be able to stop them again.

The sun creeping over the ridge revealed 2 military green Mercedes-Benz trucks pitted with bullet holes, the first truck smashed into a tree trunk and still smouldering. Scattered near and around the trucks, like the fallen leaves of trees, were many guardia, some with their helmets still on and the lifeless Galils or Garands nearby. Among the dead, the wounded guardia twisted and moaned in the dirt.

When the sun was over the horizon, Comandante Julio stood up in the creek bed and hand-signaled the compas to come down. Quincho was left with Joaquín, while Ulises, Eddy, Chele, and the other compas, safeties off on their FALs, slid down the steep embankment of the ravine, gripping branches and tree trunks to support themselves as they came down to inspect the battlefield.

Dead guardia were scattered throughout the ravine and in the dry creek; 2 were slouched over in back of the trucks where they'd been killed. The odor of scorched human hair and flesh drifted through the trucks, mixing with the sulfurous smell of gunpowder and burnt rubber. Four guardias were still alive, one of them very badly burned in the explosion when the lead truck caught fire. Parts of his uniform were burned onto his skin and were impossible to peel off. His torso and arms had the skin singed off and blistered; his bloodied face was barely recognizable as that of a human being. His loud moans had now turned to small whimpers that were fading fast.

He didn't look like he was going to make it. The other wounded they might be able to take out and treat in Sapoá or Peñas Blancas. The wounded guardia had no more fight left in them, and gladly accepted the water or cigarettes the compas offered.

Ulises inspected the cab of the second truck he'd been firing into. The cab was riddled with bullet holes, the front windows shattered and one door slightly ajar. Ulises poked his FAL into the cab, kicked the door open and looked into the face of a dead guardia sitting behind the wheel, the head thrown back against the seat, eyes and mouth open. A ring of blood had dried around the guardia's mouth; a bullet had shattered his left shoulder and 2 more had left burn holes on his chest, now soaked a deep blackish red.

The guardia's opened mouth, speaking to the void, seemed to be saying, *You did this to me and it's forever.* Ulises looked away. He'd been shooting at shadows, but if he hadn't done it, maybe a guardia would be looking at him right now, wondering how he died with his eyes open. Ulises searched around the lifeless body for weapons and found an M-16 under the seat. He quickly ran his eyes over the not yet stiff corpse sitting in the seat. Looks my age, he thought. There was something bulging in the guardia's shirt pocket. Ulises pulled it out, getting blood on his hands. He saw by the cover it was a diary with a picture of a woman partly sticking out. He briefly glanced through it without reading the details; the guardia had written of his fears and his hopes in a scrawled handwriting. He replaced the blood-soaked diary inside the shirt of the dead man. Ulises wiped his hands on the ground, mumbled something and stepped back from the truck and the dead guardia.

"Anything in there?" a compa asked him.

"No," answered Ulises. "Just this dead guardia."

"Well, give us a hand, compita, 'cause we're going to torch these sons-of-whores to hell."

Ulises helped stack the 5 dead guardias in the second truck, then a compa, using a Jerry can, poured gasoline over the bootless corpses still wearing camouflaged uniforms. Comandante Julio, carrying the deadly Browning over one shoulder, formed the squads and sent some compas on ahead with Quincho and the wounded guardia. All the captured armament was then brought together and divided amongst the remaining compas so they could carry it out. Three

Galils, two M-16s, two Garands with their clips, two .45 automatics, several crates of munitions, plus an M-79 grenade launcher. One squad was left behind to cover the ravine in case the guardia should try penetrating through there again. When the column was ready to leave, a compa struck a match to the gasoline-soaked trucks, and they burst into a yellow-orange flamed pyre, crackling and popping like pork chops in lard.

The column withdrew single-file, taking a different path out of the ravine, climbing toward the ridge, where the trees were sparse and the walking easier. The compas were tired yet exhilarated and talked animately about the combat, each one recounting several times how the bullets flew, where each placed a few on the guardia convoy, and what each one had seen. They started climbing toward higher ground, staying under the cover of trees, moving quickly, keeping an eye out for the aviation. The brushless terrain was very dry, the thin stalks of grass in this hard soil were yellowed and brittle, and the ridge on which they grew was harsh, scarred landscape. The sun, rising higher, felt like a hot yellow disk, and the heat reflecting from the earth soon had them panting and sweating. Ulises, a little deaf from the grenade explosion, eyes bloodshot and face sooty with grime and gunpowder, marched along shirtless and sweaty. He lugged his FAL on one shoulder, and strapped to his other was an M-16 with a pair of U.S.-made jungle boots tied by the laces and hanging from the barrel. Besides all that weight, he also bore the caked blood of Quincho and the face of the dead guardia. He had the rest of his life to smoke cigarettes, drink rum, and brood about the man he'd killed, but right now he felt only fatigue and nothing else.

At the peak of the ridge, as the column with Comandante Julio in the lead began its descent to Sotacaballo, Ulises turned for one last look at the place where the guardia had been ambushed. High in the blue sky, black vultures floated in circles around the thin string of grey smoke rising from the ravine.

Death of an Informer

"At 4 in the morning we attacked Cárdenas. We were 2 squads from Base 12 with orders to take the little town. The night before, we'd left the base camp in Costa Rica and marched all night led by a campesino guide.

"When we got to the lake, we prepared an ambush on the only road out of town, then, with the rest of the compas, set up a crossfire on the guardia barracks, catching the sleeping guardia by surprise; maybe they never figured we'd hit such a small town so hard. After returning a few rounds, the guardia abandoned the barracks on the run, some heading into the bush, others taking the gravel road by the lake. At daybreak we entered the empty dirt streets of Cárdenas with only a few pigs and chickens scratching around the small, thatched-roof houses. A face or 2 peeked from behind doors, then the whole town came out into the plaza, where there stood a sad-looking church.

"Our orders were to search for arms and collaborators of the dictator. We turned the houses of the Somocistas upside down. That's where I got this little .32 I have. Took it from one of the town officials—I think it was the mayor. He had it hidden in his bedroom. He was a Somocista, but we didn't do anything to him; I just confiscated his pistol.

"There was another guy we caught. He was an oreja. The village people asked for his skin; seems he had fingered several of them and some campesinos from the region. Now all those people had disappeared. Half the town followed us to his house on the outskirts of Cárdenas. The guy we were looking for wasn't expecting us. He'd been sleeping with his clothes on, so he was dressed when we got him out of bed, drunk as a pig. He was barefooted and unshaven. We confronted him with the accusations of his neighbors. In particular, an elderly woman accused him of bringing a patrol of the BECAT to her door and helping the guardia drag out her 2 sons whose mutilated bodies later appeared in a nearby ravine. He didn't deny it. In fact, he was proud of his deeds. He belonged to the Mano Blanca, he said, and he wasn't going to ask forgiveness from a bunch of sons-of-whores. That was all right with us. As an oreja we didn't care too much for him; he was a real bastard. This guy was responsible for the deaths of at least a dozen people, and here he was boasting about whom he'd turned in and taunting us that we didn't have the balls to kill him like he had done many of ours.

"Our jefe decided the death penalty was warranted in this case. He sent all the townspeople home, then ordered us to stay and witness the execution. A squad of us stood in a half-circle around the oreja in his own front room. Our jefe asked him how he would like to go. The oreja said he would like to be degollado, but doubted that there was one amongst us with the courage to do it. His eyes, red and wild, stared at each of us. We looked at each other thinking, this guy is crazy. Then one of the Panas stepped forward and said he'd be glad to do it.

"First the Pana made the oreja get down on his knees while he tied the oreja's arms behind his back and bound his feet together. When the Pana finished, he asked the oreja if he had any last words. The oreja replied, '¡Viva Somoza, hijos de puta!'

"The Pana pulled out a long, thin knife, like the kind you use to castrate pigs. I swear my legs were shaking and my knees knocking. I'd seen dead, but I'd never seen anyone killed right in front of my eyes. The Pana grabbed the oreja by the hair and pulled the head back and with one clean motion, sliced his neck from ear to ear. The oreja's eyes went big like a fish out of water, he twisted in his bindings, a terrible sound coming out of his wind pipe, blood spurting and running down the front of his shirt while the Pana held him by the hair. After an eternity, the oreja went limp. When the Pana let him go he folded into an S on the floor, his head nearly severed from the body, his eyes bulging out, and his mouth wrenched open as if frozen in the middle of an eternal, silent howl."

Heavy Weather

Shadows moved through the blacked-out town, clinging to the walls of the ruined buildings to avoid the rain. Ulises, with Fredy and Malek at the command post, a bullet in the chamber of his M-16 and the safety off, asked for the password.

"Halt—who lives?"

The reply was immediate. "Zinica."

Ulises said the countersign. "Adelante Waslala."

The group of shadows moved quickly toward Ulises. He recognized Federico by the peaked cap and the Uzi he carried. The rest of the guerrilla patrol was armed with FALs. The patrol was down from the hills with 3 prisoners dressed in civilian clothes, hatless, their hands tied behind their backs.

Federico's instructions to Ulises were brief: "Hold these men in one of your spare rooms. This one will do," he said, pointing to a room next to the command post, messy with overturned furniture. "A comandante will come in the morning to interrogate them. You must not let them speak amongst themselves." With those instructions, Federico turned around with his men and left, vanishing into the shadows and the rain.

Ulises looked at the luminous dial of his watch. 0300 hours. Ulises, Fredy, and Malek ushered the prisoners into the room Federico had indicated. It had been an office at one time; now, even in the darkness, Ulises could pick out the disordered stacks of paper scattered everywhere, the large wooden counter, the broken and upended machines, and a shattered commode. The rain continued unrelentingly into the night, pounding the bombed-out roofs of the few houses left standing in Peñas Blancas.

While Fredy and Malek covered the prisoners with their FALs, Ulises retied the prisoners' hands in front. He lit a cigarette and let them each have a few puffs, studying their faces in the cigarette's dim glow. They were in their 20s and 30s, he guessed; the oldest seemed a tough guy with a brooding, vicious face; he acted like the leader. Of the other 2, one had a flattened nose like a boxer's, and the youngest-looking one was quiet and passive. They were without jackets, their wet hair was plastered on their foreheads, and their shoes were very muddy.

The youngest one asked, "What are they going to do with us?"

"I don't know," Ulises replied, and finished the last few hits of the cigarette himself.

"You can lie down on the counter, but you cannot talk." Ulises said, and motioned for Malek to take the first watch over the prisoners. Malek sat on an empty crate and leaned back against the wall, big owl eyes very intense, his FAL cradled in front of him.

Ulises stepped outside the room with Fredy. The rain meant the trenches would be 2 or 3 feet deep in water and the compas would be in a bad way. Ulises sent Fredy to find the platoon leader to inform him of these new developments.

The guerrilla General Staff expected an all-out assault during the next 24 hours. There were only 30 some compas holding the town and half of them were teenagers like Fredy who, though he was hefty for his age, was still only 15. Everyone available was already on duty; half of them had just gone 12 hours without relief, and they would have to stay on all night and all the next day. Thirty-six hours straight without sleeping, without dropping their guard, in trenches full of cold water. Thirty compas holding the most important border outpost. "What a crazy war," laughed Ulises, giddy, gone too long without sleep. "If the guardia only knew, they'd erase us from the map!"

Through the torrential rain came the unmistakable thunder of the mortars. He glanced at his watch—quarter past. They were early tonight; the shelling was something the rain didn't stop. Usually about 0400 the guardia would hit their positions with 81mm mortars and 175mm howitzers. Tonight they must have extra shells, he thought. The incoming rounds were hitting Sapoá and from where Ulises stood, he could see the fireballs and sparks of the explosions as they landed on the little town 6 kilometers up the road. He shivered in the cold, interminable rain.

"When they drop their quota on Sapoá, they're going to switch over here," Ulises said to Malek. "When Fredy comes back, tell him to return to his post. I'll relieve you here when I finish the rounds."

Ulises then headed out toward the little creek alongside Peñas Blancas where they had trenches and foxholes. He hadn't quite reached the first trenches when the high whining *weeeee* of the incoming passed over him. It landed somewhere near the highway. Ulises sloshed into the first trench he came to, and along with 2 other compas there waited for the shelling to stop.

Jesús and Chele were in the trench trying to stay awake. Chele asked, "Any news?"

"Not really. Federico just brought us some prisoners; Malek's at the command post guarding them."

"They guardia?" asked Jesús.

"Can't tell. One of them looks pretty mean."

"Do you think they'll execute them?" asked Chele.

"I don't know."

"With our luck, they'll pick us as the firing squad."

"I hope not," said Ulises.

The conversation ended. Ulises was too numb to say much of anything else; he thought of the 5 rainy days he spent at La Calera, after the battle in the ravine, miserably wet the whole time, and the dead face of the guardia floating in the rank water of the trenches. With the first pause in the mortar barrage Ulises left Jesús and Chele and followed the path through the tall, wet grass to the other trenches and foxholes.

At 0500 Ulises returned to the command post, wet to the bone, his boots squishing water with every step. The compas in the trenches were barely holding up. He relieved Malek in the watch over the prisoners. The one with the flat nose was stretched out on the counter pretending to sleep; the other 2 were sitting on crates looking glum. One of the prisoners—the mean-looking one—stood up. Ulises casually pointed the M-16 at him, and he sat back down.

Guto, the platoon leader, and Dany the cook showed up at the command post. Ulises explained the situation to them. Guto had no news from the General Staff. The 3 of them sat before the command post waiting for the night to pass, talking of what they had done before the war. Guto wanted to go back to racing motorbikes in San José; Dany wasn't sure if he was going back to his wife and his job at the utility company or staying on in Nicaragua. Ulises just listened to the talk, every now and then interjecting something from his own experience.

At daybreak the rain slowed to a drizzle, the clouds still grey, turbulent and ominous above the land. Guto and Dany had gone away, and Ulises was glad to be alone with his thoughts. Fredy came running to Ulises looking all excited, shouting, "Ulises! Ulises, the comandante is coming for the prisoners!" The way Fredy said comandante, Ulises knew he could only mean Jacinto, the legendary commander of the Southern Front.

In a few minutes Jacinto appeared with members of his staff and bodyguards. He carried an AR 180 assault rifle with collapsible stock and wore olive greens and a faded denim applejack; fragmentation grenades were pinned to his shirt. The photos in the newspapers made him look taller than he really was.

"Where's the prisoners?" Jacinto asked.

"In this room, comandante." Ulises showed him to the room; now, in the early daylight, the true mess it was in could be clearly seen.

"What? ¡Güevones!" Jacinto shouted in a fury. Ulises immediately realized the mistake.

"But we kept them from talking, Comandante."

"¡Güevones! The prisoners should have been separated—kept in different rooms!"

Ulises was about to explain his orders from Federico, but Mesones, a Panamanian on Jacinto's staff, pulled him aside and said to him, "Don't worry. Next time you'll know."

Jacinto stepped into the room with the prisoners, and the rest of his staff crowded around him. The 3 prisoners stood up. The checked shirts and jeans they wore were streaked with mud, their unshaven and haggard faces drawn by the sleepless night.

"Bueno," Jacinto began. "We know you're guardia. If you come clean, we'll let you fellows go on the other side of the border. But, if

you try to hide it from us, it will go hard on you. You," he addressed
the mean-looking one, "what do you have to say?"

"We're campesinos. We were just trying to cross the border."

"Where are you from?"

"From San Juan."

"Do you know Doña María? La familia Ortiz? Anybody?"

"I know Juan Ortiz," the youngest prisoner spoke up, obviously
very scared of Jacinto.

"Who else?"

"That's all."

"Why aren't you boys in on the action?"

"We don't want to be on one side or the other," the mean-faced
one replied.

"And you two are campesinos, also?" Jacinto asked.

They both nodded sullenly.

Then Jacinto said to them, "Let me see your hands."

The 3 prisoners reluctantly opened their hands, palms up.

"Those hands are too soft to be campesino hands," Jacinto said.
"You boys are playing games, but we are not playing. And I'll tell you
again, it will go hard on you if you don't come clean. We know you
are orejas sent to infiltrate our lines. No one goes crossing the border
in the middle of the war zone."

"We were lost," the mean-looking one said.

"And the firing caps in your possession? And the fuses?"

"We found them."

"You all stick to this story?"

"We're campesinos," the flat-nosed one said.

"¡Pendejos! Fools! Someone who comes and fights you face to
face you can respect. But you who hide behind civilian clothes to spy
are worthless and not worthy of respect. If we capture you on the
field of battle, we treat you well and then release you, or you can join
us. Do you know what the penalty is for spies? You fools don't know
we're on the verge of victory. Our columns have just taken Granada
today. This war won't last much longer. Take them away!"

Jacinto's bodyguards moved on the prisoners, hustling them out
of the room and down the corridor toward the General Staff. Jacinto
then left in the same whirlwind in which he had arrived, surrounded
by bodyguards and staff.

The rest of the day was electric with rumors and expectation. So Granada had fallen, joining León, Estelí, Masaya, Sapoá and Peñas Blancas, flying the red and black flag of the insurrection. With Managua and Rivas under seige, the regime was breathing its last and everyone knew it. But like the dying who receive a final spasmodic burst of energy before their death, the last lunge of the enemy could be dangerous. The trench duty had to go on. In the afternoon the AC-47 gunship appeared, slow and lumbering, .50-caliber machine guns blazing from the port side, and black double-tailed pushpulls strafing the highway and the town. It rained all that afternoon on the green hills, and at night the torrential downpour came again, wanting to crumble and wash away the shattered walls.

The next morning there was news. It came with the firing of rifles along the hills, then the radio operators and the sentries outside the General Staff began firing into the air. By then everyone in Peñas Blancas knew the dictator had fled, and round after round was released in staccato bursts.

The morning was an intense high; insane jubilation mixed with a heavy sadness, a weariness that kept bringing everyone down. The firing was cut short with word to save the ammo. Everyone was still on duty till further notice. A jeep full of compas drove up from Sapoá. Six or seven compas in the back were waving and shouting, occasionally firing a round into the air. To Ulises's great joy, Armando was the driver of the jeep. "Hey, Armando! Armando!" Ulises screamed. Armando threw up his arms and ran to Ulises. They embraced each other like long-lost brothers, shouting vivas to the frente, and hugging each other again. Armando was at the mouth of the Sapoá River with a squad; these were the compas he'd brought to Peñas Blancas.

By 1000 hours the journalists from Costa Rica were swarming all over Peñas Blancas, shooting miles of film, photographing all the compas, bleary-eyed and muddy, who still wore the look of shell shock on their faces. Word was that Jacinto himself was going to give a press conference that morning.

Jacinto arrived from Costa Rica with an entourage of several jeeps and pulled up in front of the immigration building. The word immediately buzzed to all the journalists and a small crowd gathered. Ulises stood at the edge of the circle, listening. Jacinto stood

up in his jeep and looked over the crowd of journalists and compas.
Jacinto declared victory over the dictator and flung his arms out in a
V—his famous gesture—and the clicking and the whirl of cameras
went into a frenzy. Then the caravan of jeeps raced off in the
direction of Sapoá. Wachan stayed behind for the General Staff.
There was still much excitement and journalists interviewing compas about what it had been like, and the news was being shared that
Somoza had left behind a puppet ruler who still hoped to stay in
power. Suddenly the earth started shaking with the loud metal boom
of mortar explosions from a surprise barrage hitting Peñas Blancas.
The journalists went white as ghosts; the compas looked up at the
sky and ran for cover. There was a mad dash of journalists for their
jeeps and buses; incomings were landing right near the immigration
building every 2 or 3 seconds. Wachan hopped aboard the last jeep
that shrieked out of Peñas Blancas heading for Costa Rica. Indian
Joe, the Black Panamanian cook, stood in the middle of the highway shaking his fist at Wachan and cursing him as a coward. Ulises,
pressed against the asphalt parking lot in front of the duty-free store,
couldn't believe what he was seeing. "Thought Jacinto said it was
over," he muttered, his mouth full of dirt.

That afternoon Ulises sat in front of the command post cleaning
the black plastic M-16 he had captured from the guardia. The word
was that Commandante Bravo of the National Guard and 500 elite
EEBI troops were still in the hills surrounding Sapoá and Peñas
Blancas. A papaya tree near the highway was growing new branches.
He noticed how lush the grass was and the heavy overcast of the
cumulus clouds. Then he saw the 3 prisoners coming from the
direction of the border. They were walking along the edge of the
road on the far side of the highway, their hands tied behind their
backs, shoeless. They were guarded by a squad in olive green fatigues
and carrying FALs. The flat-nosed one was first, with his head
bowed down; the mean one followed with the bitterest look of any
man Ulises had ever seen. The young one was last, shuffling along in
his socks and shaking his head, mumbling, "Mamacita, ay, mamacita."

The prisoners and their escorts went beyond the general mess
hall up the road, crossed the last checkpoint past the outskirts of
town, and headed along the highway toward the rows of trees juxta-

posed on the open fields of green grass that were used for firing ranges and where herds of Brahmans wandered, freed of their pens by the war. Ulises stood up, M-16 in hand, watching the squad and the prisoners till they disappeared behind the last row of trees. He stayed for a long time searching the distant horizon, ears straining to catch the report of rifles rumbling over the hills like the turbulent grey cumulus storm clouds that had cleansed the land during the night.

Cibolca

In the cold, flat, grey-colored morning, the compas boarded 2 pickup trucks camouflaged with green and brown spray paint and with all the windows, mirrors, and headlights knocked out. They rumbled out of Sapoá, heading north on the Pan American, trying to catch the guardia at their elite training school in Cibolca. The lead truck went on 10 minutes ahead. The mejicano rode in the second truck, 2 knives in his belt, a huge machete dangling at his side and overloaded with clips. Word was the guardia had pulled out of Hill 50 and moved all the way back to Rivas. It was hard to believe they would give up the little mound of earth on the other side of the Río Ostallo. For 6 weeks the front had been stalled on that hill where the guardia were entrenched with 2 platoons and 3 .50-caliber machine guns. On the first curve of the road out of Sapoá they passed the burned-out Mercedes-Benz truck with the charred corpses of guardias in it.

Compas in the trenches near the Río Ostallo stared at them as they drove up to the sentries where the Pan American crosses over the river. The sentries waved them on. Ahead lay the open grassy terrain, the whitewashed farmhouse where Comandante Roger fell, and the hump of earth barely rising 50 feet above the flatlands where the heaviest fighting had taken place. All eyes turned to the tree line and the trenches recently abandoned by the guardia. One of the Frente platoons had just taken possession of Hill 50, and guerrillas in olive greens and red and black scarves dug around the fortifications evacuated by the retreating enemy.

Riding in the back of the truck, the wind in their faces, the compas held on to their berets and hats. On the west side of the

highway were the matorrales, the green hills, and an occasional herd
of Brahmans feeding. On the other side of the highway was the view
of the 2 volcanoes on Ometepe rising over the still lake, with grey
cloud-capped peaks like a postcard from a foreign land. Some quin-
tas along the way looked untouched by the war. The hedges were
neatly clipped, the lawn thick and very green. Where had these
people been all this time?

Approaching an open field thick with high grass, the driver
started slowing down. On the side of the road by the lake was the
military school of Cibolca, a modern 2-story red brick barracks
surrounded by coconut palms. There was a massive obstacle course
in front. This was the place where the guardia had trained with
shouts of "¡Muerte al pueblo!"

Squads from the first truck were already inside the compound,
and the sporadic popping of small arms fire could be heard coming
from within the buildings. The second truck took the driveway right
up to the front entrance and then the compas jumped out.

The compas rushed through the front gate, which had been
blasted off its hinges, searching the empty hallways and wings of the
building. Other compas ran through the rooms, shooting up suspect-
ed hiding places. There was no resistance and no guardia anywhere
in Cibolca, just the destroyed rooms where they had bunked and the
deserted dining halls turned upside down, all the windows shattered.

The repeated firing of a FAL came from behind the military
school. Everyone rushed back there to find the mejicano shooting at
a mound of green guardia uniforms and helmets they had tried to
burn before fleeing. The uniforms were piled in a large outdoor
training complex complete with an Olympic-size swimming pool.
The whitecaps of the lake came up to the cement edge of the
complex. Large pipes connected the pool to the lake to pump in
fresh water, but now the pipes were clogged and the water had
turned mossy. Hundreds of green lake frogs had fallen into the half-
filled swimming pool and, with no way of getting out, some still
swam around kicking with their big legs, but most of them were
floating belly up, drowned in the stagnant water.

Return to Sapoá

The dusty, overcrowded Flecha Azul bus from Costa Rica came to a halt in a cloud of dust and the bus driver jumped out, transit papers in hand, and headed for the command post of Sapoá. Only one passenger got off at this stop, a thickly built brown-skinned woman wearing a red print dress; a straw hat with a blue-white ribbon was perched on her head. In one hand she carried a cardboard suitcase cinched with a belt. She planted her feet firmly in the dusty earth, the straw hat shading her eyes as she squinted at the dirt plaza of the barren town.

Under the spreading branches of a giant ceiba tree a flagpole flew the Nicaraguan flag and the red and black flag of the Frente. As a child she'd played under the same ceiba, and as a young woman, 20 some years ago, the ceiba had witnessed her marriage in the plaza to that no-good husband. The black, thick-trunked ceiba had seen her children grow up and had seen her get kicked out of town by the guardia; now the same tree was welcoming her back. "Hello, ceiba," she muttered tensely under her breath, remembering when the guardia ran this town. But now they were gone, as were her children, scattered by the insurrection over the face of the land.

The driver reboarded the ancient diesel bus, ground the gears as he engaged the transmission, and rumbled out of Sapoá on the Pan American Highway. María José stood in the hot dust stirred by the departing bus. Her eyes wandered across the scarred features of her town. Craters pitted the plaza, and the nearby houses were blackened by smoke or had big holes punched in them. Dented guardia helmets rusted outside the former National Guard command post. The walls were pocked with bullet holes and spray painted with

"FSLN" and the message, MESONES PASO POR AQUÍ COMBA-TIENDO. Heavily armed compitas came and went from the command post. Somewhere a transistor radio played "Quincho Barrilete," and the lyrics mixed with the sulfurous odor of gunpowder and death that floated through the plaza.

María José dropped her suitcase on the ground and her hat on top of it. A wispy black hair curled down from her chin and she wrapped her index finger around it in a nervous gesture, contemplating what her eyes beheld; she thought of Sapoá the way it was before the war, the neighbors she got along with and the ones she didn't, the mercaderas that used to stop at her comedor on their way from Rivas to Peñas Blancas. Now she didn't see a single face she knew— just the muchachos in the plaza with their rifles that looked too big for them. An oxcart, clumsy on uneven wooden wheels, clunked down the dirt road from Sotacaballo, nearly running her over.

"¡Cho!" The thin-armed driver reined in the 2 bueyes pulling the cart. María José snapped out of her reverie and recognized the man under the weather-beaten hat. He was a campesino from the Hacienda El Tigre, up in the hills. The man also recognized María José.

"¿Yhay, María José? Long time since I've seen you in these parts."

"Maybe a few months, Justo. You have any news of my comadre Irma Raudales over by where you work?"

"She's gone. The guardia took all the campesinos from the hacienda several months ago. They said it was for questioning. Took them over by San Juan del Sur. Who knows any more about those things?"

"Why is it they didn't take you?"

The driver jumped down from his cart. The 2 bueyes were big and blond-colored with wooden yokes strapped to their horns; they were knocking against the cart and swishing their tails at flies. He patted one on the side.

"I was in Rivas with the mayordomo buying provisions. That's the only reason I escaped. Now it's just us 2 at the hacienda. He sent me into town to see if I could round up some hands." He looked around at the abandoned and burned houses. "There's a place for a cook, if you want to come, María José."

"No, thank you, Justo. You know I'm the best cook in the region, but I think I'm going to stay here in town. Maybe open up my comedor again. I don't know. I just got off the bus. Don't know if I have a house or if the guardia burned it down. I don't even know where my children are. I have to stay here in case they come looking for me."

"I understand. But you're always welcome at the hacienda."

"Thank you, Justo. Now if you'll excuse me, I must go see what's left of my place."

"Certainly, and I must see the comandante about a permit to hire workers. Good day, María."

He tipped his hat to her. She nodded slightly in return, picked up her suitcase and hat, and headed toward the big ceiba. On one side of the tree several planks were nailed together into tables and 2 large aluminum pots sat on the ashes of dead fire. She looked over the setup, making mental notes on how to improve the mess area, empty now except for a swarm of flies that covered some scraps on the dirt floor. The muchachos could use some help; 15 years running the best comedor in the region must be worth something, she thought. She continued past the mess, the burned-down houses and the houses with holes knocked in them, heading in the direction of the lake.

That ingrate Justo, she thought, following the dirt path under the palm trees that covered the ground with ochre-colored chilínco-cos. Obviously he was a conniving buzzard afraid of his own shadow and a bootlicker as well. Might even have collaborated with the guardia; time will tell. "¡Jodi'!" she exclaimed, "I have more balls than most men I've known."

On the bluff overlooking the lake muchachos did sentry duty in trenches, gazing across the calm mirror of the water and the gener-ous breast of the 2 volcanos on the horizon. María José kept on the path leading down the bluff to the lake's shore. Tiny mauve flowers, bits of broken glass, and spent cartridges littered the twisting path down the bluff.

María José kicked off her low-heeled shoes and dug her toes into the gravelly brown sand of the beach, feeling the waves of the lake splash against her feet. A flight of widgeons took off from the reeds and flew, just skimming above the water. At the foot of the bluff were hundreds of empty shell casings and remnants of more trenches camouflaged with palm fronds. A young guerrillero on the beach, his rifle shouldered, held hands with a girl in green fatigues. He was whispering something in the girl's ear that made her smile.

María José followed the foot of the bluff till she saw the charred ruins of a house, with only the blackened rafters of the roof and the door frame left standing. Next to the burned-down house stood an empty palm-thatched ramada with 3 palm trees as background. Broken tables and chairs and empty beer cans and bottles littered the ramada. A laminated Cerveza Victoria sign nailed to one beam sported several bullet holes through it.

She stopped before coming closer and stood a long time gazing at the chaos from a safe distance, not wanting to see the details, tormenting the black hair on her chin, remembering when all her neighbors had helped her build the house and the small restaurant next to it. Even the guardia had come to drink and eat at her place, and they were welcomed like everyone else. A bright green garobo eyed her quizzically from the ramada's edge as if asking, what are you doing here? Then it scampered off into the bush, its long, green tail dragging after it.

Then the pain hit her, slowly at first, then striking like a hurricane: the guardia bursting in at midnight, the interrogation with the flashlight in her eyes, the blows that followed her silence, her screams as they dragged her out, tearing her dress, the endless, tormented night that followed. She wiped away a tear clinging to her lashes. Don't be a fool, she thought, pulling herself straight, you knew what you'd find before you came back. What are you crying about? It's not worth even one tear. Not a one. She walked up to the ramada and tossed the suitcase to one side and threw the straw hat and her shoes on top of it. She pulled out the comb that held her wiry black-and-grey-streaked hair together and shook her head to let the hair flair out and hang to her shoulders.

Then she hitched the red print dress in a knot between her thick thighs and started gathering the accumulated trash in the ramada, piling it in the center of the floor, sweeping the debris up with a dried palm frond. She talked to herself as she worked: "First that no-good husband left me with 3 kids, which God knows I've done my best to raise right. A century of hardship struggling to build a life, then the guardia destroys everything, even the good memories, in one night. What's left to lose?" The thought chilled her to the bone. Time will tell, she thought, stopping to wipe the dust from her face. I'll find my children and bring them back to me. And if they're dead? I'll find them anyway. God wouldn't permit such a thing. I've had enough suffering to last a soul 10 lifetimes. "I swear," she cursed loud enough to be heard in heaven, "I will not let them ruin it all, I will not be beaten down like an animal; I'm going to raise my comedor again and people will come from all over to visit my place. I swear on my mother's grave I will."

A red sunset soon streaked the sky over the lake, and the volcanos on the island of Ometepe disappeared in the hazy, clouded light. There was no food for her but she didn't mind. Many times these past bitter months she'd been hungry, but now she was home and that was better than food. She was standing alone on the beach, pondering the waves washing over the sand, when the guerrilla couple that had been near the beach earlier came up to her.

María José was surprised at how young they were—not more than 17, either of them. It could have been one of her sons, or her daughter. She threw her arms around both of them. The young man, dark and handsome, got a little flustered; the girl took it in stride.

"What are you doing here?" the bright-eyed, round-faced girl asked, a .45 automatic bouncing on her hip.

"I used to live here; that used to be my comedor," María José gestured at the 2 squat buildings. "I built this up with my own hands and my own sweat, and the guardia destroyed it in one day. They knew how to destroy but not build. And you, where are you from?"

The young man spoke first. "I'm from Monimbó. My name's Diriangen."

"I'm Zaira. I come from Rivas, but I was at the university in León."

"Really? I have a sister in León. Her name's Aurora Mercedes. Lives in front of the plaza. They call her son Juan Chíbolas; do you know them?"

"Juan Chíbolas? Sure, we were classmates together. We're very good friends. I heard he's all right and in the provisional government," the girl said.

"God, I wish I had some beer or food for you, even just chicha," María José said.

"There's food in the comedor," offered Zaira, pointing to the bluff.

"It was you I was thinking of," María José responded, "but tomorrow or the next day, God willing, I'll haggle provisions in Rivas and you'll see what a feast I'll serve you in the evening."

"Come eat with us tonight," Zaira repeated. "Everyone in the area eats in the comedor; it's not just for us."

"Well, since you're inviting," said María José, putting on her shoes.

The 3 of them took the winding dirt path back up the bluff, Zaira leading, followed by María José and Diriangen. The washing of the waves on the lake sounded muffled and distant in the approaching twilight.

A large campfire burned beneath the ceiba tree in the plaza. Campesino families, their children huddled near them, lolled near the fire. A group of refugees from Rivas or further north, traveling on foot, had come off the highway to spend the night under the ceiba. Compitas in olive greens, FALs clinging to their backs, mingled among the civilians. Two compas were cooking a pot of rice over an open fire. Other compas turned a side of beef on a spit. The burning logs threw off hot embers that sparked up into the purple night.

María José, Zaira, and Diriangen formed the tail of the line; families with children went first. The compa serving the food, darkfaced and black-bearded, rifle on one shoulder, handed the campesino next to María José a banana leaf piled with a mound of rice and chunks of roasted meat.

"Gracias," the campesino said.

"Es del pueblo, compita," responded the compa.

The 3 of them sat down near the fires burning under the ceiba tree, too hungry to talk, digging their fingers into the rice and meat. The green lake mosquitos came out and attacked the fire and got all over the food. María José didn't mind; as a young girl growing up at the edge of Sapoá, her family ate meat maybe twice a year. It was still the same for campesino families in the hills. It felt strange being back in her home town; she hadn't seen anyone she knew, except for Justo. There wasn't a civilian in Sapoá, only refugees and the campesinos from the nearby haciendas.

Small groups of refugees sprawled near the fires, eating. One of them who sat apart from the rest wore a cowboy hat low over his eyes. After a few angry bites at the meat, he dumped the rest on the dirt. "Mierda," he cursed, "this isn't fit for a dog!" María José overheard him and noticed he didn't look worn out and shell-shocked like the other refugees. Why that big hat so low? she wondered.

The cooks removed the large pots from the fire after the last compa was fed. New logs were tossed on the dying coals, and the resurgent fire illuminated the nearby faces. The man with the cowboy hat looked up and María José clearly saw the splayed nose, the thick-lidded, glassy eyes. An ice cold hand seemed to grip her heart.

The man in the cowboy hat, sensing danger, stood up slowly and uneasily. María José jumped to her feet as if struck by lightning.

"You!" She pointed her finger right at his heart. "I know you!"

The man pinned her with a stare of his black reptilian eyes.

"You don't know me."

"Yes I do, I know you!"

"Shut up!" Then in a growl, "You're crazy, woman."

"No, I'm not crazy!"

Several people gathered around her, brought by the shouting. Diriangen and Zaira stood up, wondering what it was all about. The man tugged the cowboy hat lower and glared back at the crowd that was forming. "Where are you from?" a male voice shouted out from among the refugees.

"Who are you that I have to answer?" the man spit back.

"Are you afraid to tell us?" The voice again, taunting him.

"I'm from Rivas, all right?"

"Do you know the Martíne family who used to own a grocery near the cathedral?" the same voice asked.

"No, I don't know them. Besides, I don't have to answer this shit." The man eyed the highway from under his cowboy hat.

Diriangen casually slid the FAL from his shoulder and held it waist-high, aiming the black barrel at the cowboy's gut.

"Not so fast, compa. What's the hurry? There's no more buses for the border tonight."

The man with the cowboy hat held his tracks. The other compas near Diriangen unshouldered their weapons. Zaira unsnapped the holster cover on her .45 automatic.

"Why don't you step over here to the fire? Let's get a look at you," Diriangen said, motioning to the crowd to let the man through. Diriangen stood him next to the open flames. The man kept his hat on, his arms crossed. He wore blue jeans with a faded yellow shirt and calf-high, black rubber boots. María José, the blood pounding in her throat, walked up to him and with a quick back-hand slap knocked the cowboy hat off. A collective gasp went up when they all saw the short military crew cut.

"I knew it, I knew it!" screamed María José, pointing at him, "¡Eres guardia!"

"You don't know what you're talking about." The ex-guardia could barely control his rage. The compas gripped their rifles tightly.

"Someone get the comandante," Diriangen said.

"You're one of the guardia who . . ." María José could barely speak. "You don't remember me? You should; you held me down while I was raped."

"¡Hijo 'e puta!" the campesinos cursed. "¡Paredón!" the refugees screamed in chorus.

"You're mistaken; I'm from Rivas."

"No, you're the one that's mistaken!" that same voice in the crowd again shouted. A young, lanky figure stepped out from among the refugees. "I'm Casimiro Santos and you're Corporal Moncada of the National Guard and you took away my father, Don Casimiro Santos, from the Hacienda El Chocoyo!"

Ex-corporal Moncada focused his eyes on the worn boots of the young man.

"You can't deny it now," Casimiro Santos said. "Because I saw you do it, and many others saw you do it."

Astonishment and recognition buzzed through the crowd, as others now also identified the former guardia. The comandante appeared and after hearing the accusations ordered the man taken into custody. Two compas grabbed him by each arm to lead him away.

"Wait," María José said, "I have something I want to say to him."

The ex-corporal stood defiantly between the 2 compas. He gave María José the sideways glance of a snake who had missed its prey.

María José stepped up to his face, not knowing what she was going to do next. She looked into his eyes, saw nothing—barely a glimmer of a human being. "It's not worth it to hate someone like you. Let the people's justice take its course for the pain you've caused. But for me, it's over. The worst thing I can do to you is forgive you for what you did to me."

The ex-corporal's eyes lost the black-bead look for an instant, then turned incomprehensive, unsure, scared. María José, afraid she might start crying and confused by the emotions she had revived, turned and quickly walked away from the hushed crowd. Zaira went running after her.

"Are you all right?" Zaira asked.

"Yes, I'm fine; I just want to get back to my place."

"I'll come visit you tomorrow."

"Sure. I'll be around."

"María." Zaira stopped walking so that María José would stop also. Zaira put her hand on María's shoulder.

"Yes, my child?" María José said, looking at her.

"Oh, never mind. I'll see you tomorrow. Good night, María."

" 'Night," María José said. Zaira returned to the plaza and María José followed the path alone through the dark. The palm trees hung ominous branches in her way, blocking out the moonlight and stars. Shadows seemed to be darting in and out of the bush, and she felt a slight tingle of fear creep along her skin. The bluff and the path looked strange, foreboding, no longer what she had known or even walked on this afternoon. But she remembered where she was and knew this was her place and that the compitas were all around, dug into trenches. But Moncada's face kept following her till she reached the shoreline and headed for the ramada and the burned-down house.

María José stood before her old ramada and the charred frame of her house, the 3 palms swaying in the night, the waves soughing on the sandy beach, and she knew she could never step back into the past or rebuild her old place. Many times she had thought of revenge, what she would like to do to one of those sons-of-whores, yet when Moncada stood there guilty, her heart forgave him. She wanted to bury the pain, erase it, start all over—the right way. Her suitcase and her hat were where she'd left them. From inside the suitcase she pulled out a box of matches and a blanket that she wrapped herself in. She knew what she had to do, and painfully, almost as if in a dream, she struck a match to the pile of broken furniture, torn romance magazines, shreds of old clothing, and broken tables and chairs she'd stacked inside the ramada. The fire quickly took hold and was soon crackling, the flames licking at the purple sky. The blazing embers of the fire would rise quickly, then disappear into the black firmament. She sat by the beach under the starlit sky, gazing into the heart of the fire, her thoughts consumed by her children; Arlen in Mexico City, Ricardo somewhere, maybe the United States, and her youngest, her baby, Carlitos, who said goodbye to her one crisp September morning and went off to join the insurrection. And her comadre Irma and the campesinos from El Tigre, would they be coming back to Sapoá? Chayules, the green lake mosquitos, were flying into the fire; some would get singed and fall hissing into the flames. The trio of palms sang a melancholy adiós as the flames licked up the beams of the ramada and singed the roof, and all the dried palm fronds burst into fire, illuminating María José's round Indian face to the heavens. For the first time in years, she thought of when she was a little girl playing under the ceiba tree with Irma and Aurora Mercedes. She had been young then and full of life, and now she was starting to feel that way again, as if the whole future lay before her and within her grasp. She remembered the brilliant sunrise that used to come up over the lake and all the parties they'd had on the beach. She slapped her hips— these thighs could still keep a man busy all night if he could hold on that long, she laughed. She was glad the old place was burning; she felt no sorrow for the past that would soon be so many ashes. The face of the guardia Moncada had been the dead face of the past, and no force on heaven or earth could ever bring it back. She was anxious to start over, go for high ground. She would transplant some seedlings from the palms and build a new house and a new comedor

up there on the bluff, surrounded by a hundred palms, with a pan-
oramic, picture-postcard view of the lake and the islands of Solentiname and the 2 big breastlike volcanos in the distance, rising up
from the blue horizon.

33

A few days after his wedding, the Panamanian 33 returned to duty as head cook of the border garrison at Peñas Blancas. He stepped in one morning while Ulises was having coffee in the dining room. Ulises sometimes ate in the dining room reserved for the clerks from immigration when he didn't feel like walking up the road to the checkpoint and sitting in the crowded mess hall with flies buzzing all over his food. In here it was quiet, with just a few clerks sitting around and one or two cooks rattling pots or trying to get the gas stove working. After months of canned tuna, this converted kitchenette with the Panamanian cook 33 frying salted meat and spicing it with vinegar and peppers seemed to Ulises like the Hotel Soloy in Panama City. Ulises wasn't from immigration, but the cooks knew he had been in the thick of it, so they had his name on the list of those who could use their dining room. This was the only place to get a decent meal 2 weeks after the war because the civilians had not returned, and 33 always had something cooking and good coffee any time of the day. Ulises never asked why the Panamanian chose the name 33 and never heard him talk of the war, but he knew 33 had been with Ezequiel's column when they beseiged Rivas for 5 weeks. The Panamanian was short, stocky, with a hard look in his eyes and a permanent scowl that twisted his dark, nutmeg-colored face.

"Hey, 33," Ulises called out, "I've been sick since you left."

One of the clerks lifted his head from a plate of tuna and chopped onions.

"Yeah, it's been downhill. Glad you're back and all that."

"That dumb Tico you left in charge of the kitchen can't cook beans. I mean it literally." That was Benito, who also worked in communications. He was round, five and a half feet tall, and had a jovial personality and bushy beard.

"Yeah, I've been all right," responded 33 in his usual manner.

"How was the honeymoon?" asked Benito, putting his arm around 33's shoulder.

The clerk added on his way out, "I heard the comandante gave you 2,000 colones to live it up with and—"

33 cut the clerk short. "The fuckin' little bitch betrayed me."

All of them were stunned. The clerk halted at the door.

"O-la-la. How could that be, my friend, after that great wedding we gave you?" asked Benito, his arm still on 33's shoulder.

"Yes, she betrayed me, damn it!" 33 looked sullenly at Ulises and sat down at the small table he occupied. Benito stood behind 33. The second cook preparing some food on the far side of the room perked up.

"It didn't last 48 stinkin' hours," 33 said bitterly. "She tells me she loves another. Can you believe that? ¡Puta madre! Man, I wanted to kill her, hurt her like she did me. Why does she do this? Forty-eight hours and that was it. I threw her out. I said, here, take your things and get the fuck out."

"Oh man, you mean she turned on you?" Benito was tickled by this. "My God!"

"She did me wrong," 33 said, looking at Ulises but asking for no condolences.

"But why? What happened?" Ulises asked him.

"It just happened, brother. She can't be trusted. She took a set of cologne and some money. Like a common prostitute. That's what I think of her."

Benito said, "Compa, they took you for a ride."

"Is she Nica?" It was the cook on the other side of the dining room and the clerk who had been on his way out who now came over to listen.

"No, she's Costa Rican. But she can't come in here anymore. She's banned. She made fun of all of us—our traditions, our way of life. She married me here army-style, swore by these guns we fought with, this is our way. But she loves another, she says." 33 slapped his palm down hard on the table. "¡Puta madre! I'm not going to abandon my post for some slut. I told her that in San José. I'm going back like I said I was, you can do what you want. Ezequiel had asked me who I was marrying. When I told him, he warned me she was a bad woman, but I went ahead, anyway."

"Should've listened, compa, then you wouldn't have those funny horns growing out of your head." Benito laughed at his own joke, but no one else did.

"But you didn't tell us what happened," said the second cook in his T-shirt and apron.

"She loves another," 33 said.

"But are you sure?"

"She told me."

"How? When?"

"Well, after we got a room in San José, you know, I was feeling real good. She suggested we go to a disco to have some drinks. And that's when I found out what she really was."

"But what did she do?"

33 took his eyes off Ulises and turned around to see who was asking so many questions. The second cook backed off. Then 33 continued.

"She went to see this guy at the bar. They talk, she dances with him and pretty soon he has his arms around her and she lets him— and then—God damn everything—if she comes back here again I'll have her arrested and she knows it," he said, raising his index finger to emphasize the point. "That whore was kissing the dude right in front of me. Man, by the time I dragged her back to the hotel I was so drunk I couldn't even talk."

"Are you sure you saw all this?" asked Ulises.

"Fuckin' straight. I got her and said, 'Come on, you little whore,'" and 33 made a pantomime like when a man mounts a woman. "I got her like this, her leg up on a chair and gave it to her good, made her sore. Man, when this rider was finished I had worked up a good sweat. The bitch couldn't hardly move."

"Damn, 33, you did all right," Benito congratulated him.

33 smiled bitterly. "You're damn right. No whore does that to me. I asked her why she did it, you know in the disco? And she comes out with some shit about how that's her ex-boyfriend and she realized she still loved him. What shit!"

"Did you hit her?" the second cook wanted to know.

"No," replied 33 quickly, "it's against a man's honor to hit a defenseless woman."

"That's my man," said Benito, repressing a chuckle.

"But I left her there. Had to leave her. Left the keys to the room, everything. Went walking downtown and one of those putas gives me the come-on when she sees my uniform. Tells me, 'Come on, I'll give you a free one. I like guerrilleros.'" 33 made a motion with his hands like stopping a cork in a bottle and smiled. "We did it all night. If you've never eaten that good stuff . . . I drove her crazy." The second cook got flushed. "Then I went to the security house in Liberia and told the person in charge, Dr. Ramírez, what happened. Showed him the marriage certificate signed by the comandante and 21 compañeros in arms. Told him it was invalid. He agreed to take it off the rolls. Then she has the nerve to show up at the house. I told the doctor not to let her sleep inside. Let her sleep outside in the back yard, on the dirt, so she knows how it feels. The next morning she got up real quiet-like. That's the last I saw of her. Like I said, she can't come into this country anymore. They'll throw her in jail. That's why we fought, wasn't it? To throw the trash out. You know what you do with women like her in Panamá? You slice their face with a straight razor, that's what you do, or you slice their ass. That way she's marked for life. When another man sees it, he knows what it means. She's got a knife scar on her ass. In Panamá that means this woman betrayed another man."

33 got up with a disgusted look on his face. "Shit, what a life. But what can you do? You gotta keep working. But that's what you do to women like that. A woman with a slice in her ass knows it's going to be hard to find another man 'cause the man's gonna know she's a tramp. One with a sliced face has only street walking left for her." He lit a cigarette. "Damn," he muttered, "it's getting late, I'll see you guys around. I gotta start moving the machinery here so I can cook up some lunch." And he left.

The group around 33 broke up. Ulises finished his coffee, went outside and washed the metal cup in a tub of a soapy water and rinsed it out with the only working faucet in town. Far away on the horizon between the burnt-out shells of buildings, he could see the volcano Maderas with white puffs of smoke around its peak. It was a little past 8 in the morning and the sun was rising over the border crossing on the Pan American Highway; he had work to do. What lousy luck, thought Ulises, walking across the highway to the bombed-out store that served as the communications office, with the rough verdant hills in the background. At 33's wedding with the Tica, they'd made a processional arch with their FALs under which the couple passed into matrimony. Then, whisky that they'd captured from the duty-free store during the offensive was passed around and they were able to sample it for the first time. The comandante gave them both leave and money. Everybody was happy. Afterwards the compas sat around a campfire and sang songs and talked all night. It was hard, right after the war, when you were recovering from all the fighting and death to get burned like that. It could easily break a man inside. If 33 wasn't too wrapped up with her, he'd bounce back. If he was tough in the heart he'd survive. He seemed all right now. What Ulises saw bothering him was the loss of face, of honor, here amongst soldiers, survivors of war—33 had been hustled by a woman for a few days in a hotel and some bottles of cheap cologne. It was tough.

The next couple of days Ulises noticed 33 talking as usual at one of the tables, but mostly with men returning to the country; he never talked much with women. Just said hello and that was it. At night, he'd get out a guitar and sit in front of the dining room with a candle for light and sing painful boleros, as if he was trying to get her out of his system.

But each day 33 seemed to be less involved in what was going on. New phone cables were being installed and the electricity would be hooked up in a week, but to him it didn't matter. More and more, 33 delegated authority to the second cook—a good Tico, but nothing compared to 33, who still had to explain how to strip the meat from the carcass, salt it, and hang it up to dry on the barbed-wire fence to preserve it. 33 carried a deep, sullen bitterness, but didn't let you see it. On the surface he was the same. Ulises caught him downfaced a few times, and 33 looked away quickly.

Then one morning Ulises came in the dining room and noticed that the coffee tasted muddy and that the Tico cook was preparing canned tuna and onions for breakfast. Ulises didn't have to ask. There was a definite feeling of 33's absence in the dining room. The change seemed permanent. That afternoon Ulises noticed the Tico cook by the faucet rinsing some very dark-colored meat that looked way past its prime. Ulises felt in his pocket for the paregoric pills he was taking for stomach pains. When I get hungry today, Ulises said to himself, think I'll take a stroll and try the general mess hall up the road.

The Dead Who Never Die

"Carlos Fonseca is of the dead who never die."
—Tomás Borge

The red taillights of the pickup truck faded into the obscurity of the jungle night. Ulises tucked the brown paper bag under one arm and started along the center of the road in the direction of Nicaragua. The two beers in La Cruz gave him a slight buzz that he carried with him through the darkness. He'd been lucky to catch a ride outside La Cruz from the Tico who'd taken him as far as no-man's-land, that strip along the Nicaraguan border abandoned by the Costa Ricans. Peñas Blancas was a 5-kilometer walk, the driver had said when he dropped Ulises off. The road was unlit and without traffic along this stretch of highway that cut a cleft through the lush mountainside buzzing with dipterous insects and flashing fireflies. Black, inky clouds full of thunder blotted out the sky. Giant guanacaste trees stretched grotesque limbs, and vague shadows darted in and out of the mysterious, mist-draped tropical terrain.

A half hour later he recognized the peaked shadow of the abandoned Costa Rican aduana through the cover of trees. The first night, when entering Nicaragua with a column of 150 compas, Ulises had slept under the sloping roof of the customs house. He stopped to rest near the same spot. There was no sign of any living creature except perhaps the iguanas that scurried away in a rustling of branches as he approached. Ulises could hear them but not see them. After a few minutes he continued on the road, and soon a light appeared burning in the distance. Could it be? he wondered. Is that the glow of an electric light? With quickened step and heart

103

beating faster, he hurried on the last 500 meters till he could make out the ruins of what had been the border town of Peñas Blancas.

A cold, stiff wind stirred the guanacaste trees along the highway as Ulises reached the imaginary borderline that separated Costa Rica and Nicaragua. The needle was horizontal across the road. Ulises identified himself to the compas at the sentry box, keeping the brown bag stashed under his arm; they lifted the needle and he crossed over into Nicaragua. A ditch ran under the highway some 50 meters from the border; to his left were the remnants of sandbags that had been the pit for the .50 they used to ward off air attacks. A little farther beyond, the silhouette of Peñas Blancas was fixed against the black sky. The Nicaraguan flag and the Frente flag flapped in the night wind before the low-roofed duty-free store, now converted to a communications center filled with radio equipment instead of imported spirits. Behind the communications center stood the biggest building at this border station, where the glow of electric lights was being seen for the first time. Ulises stopped to admire the string of 6 low wattage light bulbs swaying before the one-story peaked roof of the immigration building. Two compas in full gear beneath the pale glow stood a casual sentry. Ulises had never seen any light in this town. During the months of the war, it had been prohibited to expose any light—even a match—that might reveal a position to enemy sharpshooters. Ulises felt good that the lights were on tonight, then he felt funny for enjoying some light bulbs glowing in the dark.

Behind the immigration building everything was still as it had been; the brick barracks and the warehouses, the little cemetery with handmade crosses and the backdrop of night that buried the trees and hills beyond.

Peñas Blancas was an immigration building on one side of the highway and a one-block strip of stores and restaurants on the other side. All the civilians had fled during the war; the stores and restaurants that had been the heart of town were completely gutted, ransacked, and bombed. The civilians had not returned, except for the mercaderas who came from Rivas to sell vigorón to the bus passengers headed for Managua who stopped at the immigration building to have their papers checked. All the former import stores of the dictator were now offices for the new army and government.

Ulises crossed the highway to the single block of shops and civilian dwellings. In one of those buildings a light also burned.

Ulises looked in through a broken window; many compas were gathered inside, talking animatedly under the glare of a single light bulb. Some 15 men and women in various types of olive green uniform occupied 3 tables. Against one wall rested an assortment of FALs, Galils, and M-16s. Ulises pushed open the door and a cheer rose up when they saw him enter. Everyone greeted him with a hello or a slap on the shoulder. The room was a mixture of Nicaraguans and Costa Ricans, Panamanians, Colombians, even Europeans. He was another internationalist, spoke good Spanish and English, and was as pinolero as any Indian from Masaya.

Venancia, the zarco-eyed girl from Matagalpa with tight curly hair and coffee-colored skin, was the last to approach him.

"Saludos, compa, when did you get back?"

"Just now."

"How was your one-day pass in La Cruz?"

"Wild," he said and saw a flicker of a smile on Venancia's face. "I see they got the electricity together in time for our little celebration."

"They finished about 5."

"I brought something for you. Would you like to have it now?"

"Save it for later," she said. "What else did you bring?"

The other compas gathered around him now asking the same question.

"I have come through," Ulises said, unwrapping the brown paper bag and revealing 2 pints of whisky to loud and hearty cheers. He also pulled out a box of .38-caliber bullets for the pistol Leoncito had, for which they had not a single round. Leoncito's furrowed face lit up like a kid's at a party.

"Let the fiesta begin!" shouted big-bellied Benito, his round face smiling as he gripped an amber bottle with his big hands. He twisted the cap off and poured himself a drink that he quickly downed. The bottle passed from hand to hand, each one carefully taking a capful.

Ulises watched as the whisky was poured—Malek from Bluefields, black Cleto from Corn Island, el chele from Colombia—getting ready for their little party. Leoncito was smoking intensely while flaco Armando stood at the long counter with black-haired

Ruth and Venancia, sharing a capful. A large white sheet painted with slogans that Ulises had been doing for a campesino rally in Rivas hung on one wall. The large, wide room of the former restaurant had a fan in the high ceiling that didn't work. Behind the main room was a smaller room overlooking a patio where Ulises slept. He'd been the one chosen to go to La Cruz for the whisky; during the war they shared everything. This drink would be as good as any he would have in his life.

Malek, the Arab-Nica from the coast, was the master of ceremonies for the inaugural of what they planned as the new cultural-political center of Peñas Blancas. Malek began with a short speech in Bluefields English; then, accompanying himself on acoustic guitar, he launched into a couple of Nicaraguan maypole songs from the Atlantic coast. Malek closed his set with a Cat Stevens number. The audience of compas applauded heartily and cheered while Malek took a long bow. Some of the compitas leaned against the walls; others sat cross-legged on the floor, a nice glow around them. Ulises, standing at the back of the room, felt a sudden rise of happiness brought on by the whisky.

"Compas y compitas," Malek continued, "ahora es nuestro gran placer, it is now a pleasure to introduce the poet of the Southern Front, Leoncito!"

Leoncito, a short, tough man from the port of Corinto, 21 years old, limped forward. He had brought the guitar from Sapoá for tonight; in his right leg he carried shrapnel from El Naranjo. He asked for another capful before beginning. Benito, the keeper of the spirits, passed him the half-full bottle, and León took his share, then passed it around. Venancia drank next to last, then handed the nearly empty pint to Ulises. There was a corner of amber liquid left that he downed. The spirits burned his throat, warming his body from the inside out. He couldn't help smiling at Venancia and she returned a smile with her sparkling green eyes. Ulises felt the glassine envelope with the tiny white carved flower earrings in his shirt pocket.

Leoncito recited a poem by Tomás Borge about the bourgeoisie. Everyone applauded his gutsy performance. Leoncito loved the ovation and recited another poem—shorter this time—his own and not as good. Everyone applauded anyway.

Next Malek introduced, with a flurry of imaginary trumpets, a Basque compa who'd come to fight in the insurrection. Blas stepped forward and offered a song from his native land, sung in Euskara. Though no one understood Euskara, it was an upbeat, rhythmic song and they all joined in with hand-clapping. When Blas finished, everyone asked for another song. That was the only one Blas knew, so that finished that.

The room had become warm with the exhilaration of the party, and the whisky had everyone in a good mood. Ulises put his arm casually around Venancia's shoulder, and she, with an ever-so-slight movement, made his hand slide off. Ulises stood straight then, his hands stuffed in his back pocket. Malek, now joking with the audience, borrowed a pair of sunglasses and, mimicking a microphone in one hand, was doing a fabulous imitation of a nightclub emcee. The only thing missing was a spotlight. Malek introduced Juana and Elías from Monimbó. They stood in front of the group and said a few words about their barrio and the insurrection of September. There was a clearing of throats when Juana and Elías dedicated their song to their barrio in Masaya. They sang "Vivirás Monimbó," and when they came to the chorus that Ulises loved so much, he heard the first drops of rain begin falling on the roof. It began softly, but in a minute he could tell it was a full-fledged storm that was breaking.

The evening went on and no one paid attention to the rain, least of all Malek, deep into his hipster emcee role. Malek called on Venancia but she declined to come forward, with an apology for not being an artist or performer. Malek kidded her from his make-believe cabaret stage and looked around for someone else to perform. Ulises was thinking maybe he would recite a short poem about California, but it was half in English. It wouldn't be as good a performance as Leoncito's but it was all he knew by heart. He rehearsed the lines mentally to see if he remembered it all.

As if reading his mind, Malek called on him to step forward. Ulises accepted the invitation, stepping to the front of the room with the confidence that being a little high gave him. He was about to begin the poem when the door swung open and Angel stepped in from the rain. Water dripped on the floor from Angel's parka, his FAL was slung over one shoulder and the barrel tip was wrapped in plastic. His face was ghostly in the weak light, his eyes shaded by the visor of his cap. A steely silence came in with Angel. He spoke in his normal tone, but his words carried across the room.

"They found a dead compa near Sotacaballo, his throat cut. We just brought him in right now." Angel's words hung in the air, taking the life out of the party and leaving only a dead silence and the echo of the rain that could be seen behind the open door where Angel stood. Anger rose in everyone's faces as easily as the whisky had done a little while before.

"The bastards!" Benito cursed under his breath.

"There's general formation in front of the immigration building right now. The comandante will say a few words, then we will form an honor guard till the burial in the morning. So let's get going." Angel turned back into the rain and crossed the 2-laned Pan American Highway to the immigration building.

The party broke up immediately. The compas put on their gear and berets, slung rifles on their shoulders, and filed out into the darkness of the rain and night. Ulises left last, waiting for everyone to clear out. Then he shouldered his M-16, turned off the light, and closed the door as he left. The rain hit him hard and cold in the face, running down his cheeks and neck. Before he was across the highway he was wet to his bones.

The string of lights illuminating the entrance to the immigration building was swinging back and forth. The compas who weren't on duty were forming in front of a large munitions crate resting on top of a table. A pair of feet stuck out of the crate from under a black plastic sheet. Someone pulled back the plastic that covered the body. Several compas looked at the dead man. No one seemed to know him. Ulises didn't take a look. He'd seen the dead guardia in the burned-up truck outside Peñas Blancas, the bodies bloated by the tropic sun and covered with flies. The stench that hit you like a wall. There was no curiosity about the dead after that.

In groups of twos and threes and alone, compas were coming in from the barracks, stepping out of the darkness and into the pale glow of the light, where their features were revealed. Eyes etched with sleepless nights, skin burned by the sun; some had beards, some long hair, and they wore an eclectic collection of uniforms, hats, and rifles. Soon there were 30 or more compas around the wooden box. The comandante appeared, his face drawn and his khaki uniform dark with water. A .45 was strapped at his side. Ulises felt the tension in the group as the comandante addressed them, hands behind his back, voice low yet resolute.

"Compañeros. We're here tonight to mourn one of our own. This compa, missing nearly a week, was found today tied to a tree. He had been tortured and killed by the guardia escaping into Costa Rica. His pseudonym was Manuel. We don't know his real name, but that doesn't matter. Maybe he wasn't even Nicaraguan; that doesn't matter, either. What matters is that he fought for the liberation of our people. What matters is that he never turned back. He sacrificed his life so that we could be free of hunger and ignorance and the exploitation of man by man. He is as much a martyr of our homeland as the compas who died in the heat of the insurrection with a battle cry on their lips. That his death comes after the triumph makes it all the more tragic and shows us that the enemy will stop at nothing in his frenzy to disrupt our vanguard and our people from the road we have chosen.

"The blood of compañero Manuel, like the blood of so many others, was not spilled in vain. In a way, our cause and our country have been consecrated by their sacrifice. Now it is up to us, the living, to carry on until the final victory, compañeros. There will be an honor guard around compañero Manuel's body until morning, when he will be buried with military honors. Compañero Angel will pick a squad to stand the first watch. You may now fire a volley in salute to the fallen guerrillero."

The compas aimed rifles at the heavens and the stars. A volley of automatic fire burst like thunder. Ulises squeezed off several rounds, the flash of fire shooting out the muzzle of the M-16. Then the shooting stopped and a shout rose from one throat and everyone else responded, "Long live the heros and martyrs!"

"¡Compañero Manuel!"

"¡Presente!"

"¡Patria libre!"

"¡O morir!"

The great volcano of emotion vanquished the night and the rain, but Ulises became aware of it again, the night surrounding him and the rain sinking into his shoulders.

Angel picked Ulises, Malek, Venancia and 3 others for the first watch. They stood 3 on each side of the makeshift coffin, at a soft attention, eyes forward. Ulises, at the end of a row, could see Venancia out the corner of his eye, at the opposite end of the other row. She stared ahead, shoulders back, Galil strapped high. Ulises wondered about her. She had been a source of torment and pleasure for him since she appeared at the front with her country-folk sensuality. She was of the crew that manned the shortwave radio in the sand-bagged basement that served as the General Staff of the Southern Front. Venancia was popular and several men were courting her, though she seemed to have stayed clear of entanglements. He would like to know her better; there were rumors of a boyfriend, but he didn't know if they were true. How stupid, thought Ulises, to be thinking like that of a woman while standing duty over a compañero. The corpse of a compañero, he corrected himself. Even if it wasn't much of an honor guard, in a nearly abandoned border outpost that no one would ever recall as vividly as those who fought for it and saw comrades die for it, he had to do it right. He shoved aside all thoughts of the white carved-flower earrings; it didn't matter whether he would ever give them to Venancia or not. Somehow, he knew this incredible loneliness and yearning he carried inside would not be eased tonight. He was afraid Venancia with her green doe eyes would never be the one to hold him to her breast.

The minutes passed, each one accounted for in a timeless journal that no longer mattered to the dead. Ulises thought of the rain falling on all the little crosses that were planted behind the big warehouse. He thought of the mothers and fathers who had appeared in Peñas Blancas asking the whereabouts of their sons and daughters. Often the journey ended behind the warehouse in the small, improvised cemetery with handmade crosses and a name— sometimes just a pseudonym—painted on them.

There was one case in particular that had moved Ulises. A woman arrived one crisp morning a few days after the war, searching for her son. She was in her 40s, her face worn and haggard, a thin coat of dust covered her simple black dress. She'd come from Chinandega to Peñas Blancas. Ulises was on duty that day in the former store that housed the political commission.

Doña Mary showed Ulises a letter that her son had written her. Ulises gave her his chair and read the letter standing up. It was written in pencil, in simple handwriting on blue-lined paper that had been folded over many times. The son was saying good-by, telling her of his decision to join the Southern Front. She was alone in the world, she said, when Ulises finished reading the letter. Her son had been everything—he must still be alive, no? Could Ulises help find him?

Ulises pulled out pad and pencil to jot down notes. Doña Mary described her son while recounting the story of her journey. First she'd gone to Managua to inquire of the General Staff of the Army. They informed her there was no trace of him in Managua, but that he might be in Rivas or Sapoá. She went looking for him and in Sapoá met some compas who knew him and had been with him, but they were unable to say where he was now. With her heart full of hope she walked the 6 kilometers from Sapoá to Peñas Blancas; surely he would be here. Ulises brought her a glass of water from the faucet outside which she drank down and thanked him. She sat back stiffly in the chair when she was finished. Her face was still flushed, and she wiped her forehead with a blue handkerchief she pulled out of a pocket in her dress. Ulises put his notepad away, and Doña Mary folded her hands on her lap.

Ulises went out into the scorching midday sun and crossed the 2-lane highway. He went to each of the different staffs with the description and name. He got nothing from Communications or the Quartermaster. But at Security he heard the story from a compa who had been at El Ostional. Her son's pseudonym was Marcos; when the order came to pull back from El Ostional, he volunteered to cover the retreat. The compa from Security had helped recover the body a few days ago; Marcos was buried in the little cemetery behind the warehouse.

Doña Mary was still sitting in the chair, her head back and eyes closed, when Ulises returned. She opened her eyes and the first thing she did was smile at Ulises, full of hope and expectation. Ulises didn't know how to tell her; he just said that maybe they should take a walk.

They went out together into the bright sun. In front of the immigration building there was a blue bus with a white horizontal stripe that was going to Managua. The bus driver had pulled in under the portals and the passengers coming from Costa Rica were disembarking for customs. As they came into the busy immigration building full of people behind counters typing, people with suitcases and passports waiting to be stamped, and children shouting and crying, Doña Mary seemed to breathe hope at the life around her. Ulises realized that she thought her son worked here, but they continued out the other end of the building and kept going past the warehouse. Ulises kept quiet till they turned the corner of the warehouse. Then he was going to say something, but they were already in front of the little cemetery and Doña Mary gasped when she saw the little crosses and heard Ulises saying, "He was at El Ostional. We think he's buried here. We have to look."

"Ay, Dios mío," she sighed, "Dios mío. I prayed, oh how I prayed." After a few moments, she pulled herself together and said it was better to know the truth than to be in doubt.

There were some 30 crosses arranged in a haphazard manner. They looked at them together, starting with the ones in front. When they got near the end, she found her son's name painted on a wooden cross, and beneath that his pseudonym and a date, 6-6-79.

Yes, somehow in her heart she had known he was dead. A mother's instinct had led her here, and she had to know, she said between tears that flowed freely down her face. He died doing what he wanted, fighting for what he believed in. His death was not in vain; her words came mingled with her sobbing. Ulises stood at her side, his arm around her shoulder till she finished crying. So many young people, she said as they were leaving, so many of them dead.

They walked back in silence past the warehouse and around the immigration building. She thanked Ulises for everything and said she was going to pick a few wildflowers to leave on his grave, then probably take the bus to Managua this afternoon, from there to Chinandega. Her business was finished here. Before she left, she asked of Ulises the only favor a mother could ask of a stranger, "Please keep my son's grave clean."

That had been last week; now here he was again, watching over the dead. And what good were the dead, he thought, if they had not died for the living? And what good were the living, if they didn't keep the memory of the dead?

After a while, Ulises shifted his stand, resting the rifle butt on the ground, his hands wrapped around the barrel. Angel came by and disappeared again into the shadows. The rain kept falling; sometimes a wind would whip it around so that it sprayed their backs and necks. Ulises could live with it. He had spent nights in trenches filled with rain, had learned to sleep knee-high in water. At the limestone quarry La Calera it had been a week on a barren ridge, without cover—not even plastic sheets—and it had rained every day. You got used to never being dry, sleeping in mud, never taking your boots off till your feet began to rot. The rain was never, ever, that bad again for Ulises.

The memories of La Calera dredged up other images, which came faster and in increasing numbers, bubbling up from his subconscious with all the dead floating to the surface. The face of the guardia killed in the ambush outside Sotacaballo appeared before his eyes. The guardia was maybe 27 or 28. He must have had relatives and a girlfriend somewhere to mourn him. Ulises had dragged him out of the truck and had found the blood-stained diary on the body. To have read it would have been a greater offense. So he left it on the corpse. Still, the dead face of the guardia stared at him through many nights. In the end he shook it off, but he would always carry the dead: Rubén Salazar dead in East Los, his barrio homeboys lost in Nam, and who could ever forget Toño? Brave young Toño. A born warrior and leader, with that incredible seriousness in one so young. Toño doing Wing Chun at Ocean Beach to prepare for the war. Ulises recalled the first rumor of Toño's death, which was false. Then months later, again came the news that Toño had fallen. This time it was true. Toño had been driving a jeep to the front with one leg in a cast. He was in a fury at Jacinto and was going to straighten out the problems, driving recklessly, full of guaro, the jeep out of control, overturning, flipping end over end. Ulises was glad to see Armando and Venancia in the room; he had heard that Kike, Chombo, and Willie had made it, and that Santos, Juan, and Fern were still alive. But sometimes he missed the dead something awful, and it was moments like this that the dead filed before him, singly and en masse.

The rain slowed down and the shift in the wind could be seen in the raindrops changing course and in the swaying of the string of lights over the coffin. It seemed to Ulises that each raindrop falling in the glow of the light was the name of one of the dead. Legends like Carlos Fonseca, Germán Pomares, Pedrito Arrauz, and Eduardo Contreras; names that would live forever like Arlen Siú, Leonel Rugama, and Julio Buitrago. You could keep counting back to Rigoberto López Pérez, Augusto Sandino, and Farabundo Martí, and yes, Emiliano Zapata, and ever further back to Anastasio Aquino, Francisco Morazán, Lempira, Diriangen, and Cuauhtemoc, till every raindrop was the name of a fallen comrade, warrior, poet, or worker. It was a lot of spilled blood to be accountable to; a lot of dying had gone into this triumph for the living. The immense roll call of the dead made him stand up straighter.

Ulises could tell the watch would soon be over, and he stopped counting the names of the fallen ones and just waited firmly, his eyes wandering across the features of the other compas, their emotions much like his, drained by the sleepless nights, the endless rains, and the war.

Angel reappeared with more men. The compas had that look of the half-living, their eyes bleary red, their faces unshaven and wet; some had draped a sheet of black plastic around their shoulders. They changed the guard. It was the early morning hour of a new day and the rain kept falling hard and interminably. After they were relieved, Ulises offered Venancia a cigarette and they both stood under the portals of the immigration building while he fished out some smokes from a plastic Baggie. They smoked in silence while the other compas stood guard over the dead man.

During a pause in the rain Ulises and Venancia made a break for the barracks where she was billeted, splashing through the puddles in the dark. Ulises followed her shadow till they came to the short, square buildings edged with the ambiguous shape of trees. A captured guardia 175-mm howitzer with a plug in the barrel squatted next to her barracks.

Under the safety of a small porch, Venancia pulled up, breathing hard. Ulises followed close behind, stopping when he came up against her body. He was panting from the run, and he laughed in her ear, his mouth wet from the rain.

"I haven't had this much fun in the rain since I was a kid."

Venancia laughed. "Poor Ulises, he's all wet."

He supported himself against the door with one hand, his rifle behind his back, barrel down, pressing close to Venancia so he could see her face in the dark and imagine her red lips, like the coffee of Matagalpa in the harvest season.

"I have something for you," he said.

"That's nice of you. But I can't accept it."

"You don't even know what it is."

"It doesn't matter. It's the thought that counts. Isn't that what they say? But thank you, anyway."

"It's a pair of deer bone earrings carved with beautiful flowers that I brought you from La Cruz."

"Why did you do that, Ulises?"

"Because I thought you were someone special."

There was only silence; the rain was playing a trick—seeming to fade away, only to come back harder in a few minutes. Ulises felt the tenseness in Venancia. He pulled back and now could only see the shadow outline of her face. He touched her shoulder.

"What's the matter?"

"Nothing."

"Won't you take the earrings?"

"I can't."

"Why not?"

"I don't want any sentimental gifts from anyone."

"What's wrong with a gift to someone you like very much?"

"No, Ulises, you must not think of me like that. You must not grow fond of me because I will not grow fond of you."

"Is it something I've done?"

"It's not you, it's me. I promised myself I wouldn't get involved with anyone, not for a long time anyway. You see, I was very much in love once, actually married for 2 weeks."

"What happened?"

"He was killed here in Peñas Blancas. Shrapnel hit him in the heart. A tiny, tiny hole through his heart." Her voice wept.

"I didn't know."

"He died in my arms."

"I'm sorry."

"It's all right. It's not your fault. He wanted to be an architect, to build things. He was the gentlest man I've ever known. He's still so

much a part of me, it's like he's with me every day. I don't want to
believe he's dead. I'm going to stay with his family in Rivas next
week."

In the deathly still of the night, the rain picked up its tempo,
first a few drops, then more and more hitting hard on the little
porch roof. The wind was cold and swirling around them.

"As a friend to a friend," Ulises said, pressing the glassine envelope with the carved flower earrings into her hands, "accept this
from me."

"As a compañera from a compañero, I will," she said.

"Good night, Venancia."

"Good night, compita."

She slipped into the unlit barracks, and he stood for a moment
on the little porch watching the rain fall in a drizzle. Then he
walked back to his room through the shadows of the bombed-out
border town. The rain no longer fazed him; he was as stiff and cold as
he could get, carrying a dead man's weight on his back.

The electric glow from the immigration building guided him
away from Venancia's barracks. Its illumination was the only light
for miles around. Six compas guarded the remains of compañero
Manuel beneath the portals as the wind blew the string of light bulbs
back and forth.

Ulises skirted the immigration building, staying under the trees,
and crossed the paved 2-lane highway that Peñas Blancas straddled.
The 10 or so low-roofed buildings near the highway were in ruins.
All the import offices, duty-free stores, warehouses, houses, and
restaurants were turned inside out, scattered away by the war. Roofs
were caved in and there were holes in the walls. Only one water
faucet worked in the whole town and nothing else.

Ulises stepped under the arcade that connected the string of
storefronts and went past the sleeping quarters of the new police
force; a sentry sitting outside cradled an Uzi on his lap. A few
shattered doors down was the community room where they had
gathered earlier. Inside the empty restaurant only the lifeless forms
of the long counter and the tables and chairs could be made out; he
didn't turn on the light. He stepped around the chairs and to the
back door feeling his way through a short, narrow hallway, then
came into a small room. This had been the pantry of the former

restaurant; he had cleaned it out and washed down the walls. Now he kept his cot here for sleeping.

Ulises crouched down and with his fingers felt for a candle stuck in a bottle and a matchbook. He struck the match to light the candle. The wick sputtered momentarily in his cupped hands before gaining strength and blossoming into a nice yellow flame. A mound of dead chayules, little lake mosquitos, was piled high around the candle, burned by the light that had attracted them. Ulises watched the candle till he was sure it wouldn't go out. The black M-16 was placed next to the cot. He removed his boots and socks, feeling the jungle rot scars on his feet. He laid aside his Swiss knife and watch, then undressed quickly, putting his wet jeans, khaki shirt, and boots to one side, and rubbed himself dry with a blanket. From under his cot he pulled out a pair of fatigue pants and an olive green T-shirt that he put on. He was lucky to have this space; it was nothing to boast of, but it beat the barracks. He'd even found some books in the ruins, the *Odyssey* and *Cien años de soledad,* and a candle; this was the height of luxury. In the morning his view was of an unkept garden and a wall covered with vines and tiny mauve flowers. Beyond that were the green hills of Nicaragua. It was all right, he thought, sitting down on the cot, his bare feet on the brick floor. He wasn't complaining after sleeping in the mud and rain.

After blowing out the candle, he got onto the cot and pulled the blanket over him. But he couldn't fall asleep; his mind kept repeating the incident with the earrings, the fiesta that had started the evening, and the guard duty over the fallen compañero. Venancia had helped him save face by accepting the earrings; he probably wouldn't see her again after next week. She didn't need all the bullshit; she'd had her one great love and that was enough. His attempt at seduction didn't make things any better. He suddenly felt like a fool. How was it he hadn't known before? Obviously he wasn't paying attention. A dead husband, Jesus, married only 2 weeks. What a moment to find out. He figured it was the loneliness, that unbearable, fathomless, hermetic, uncrossable ocean of solitude, that had him in a bad way. The little fiesta had broken the spell temporarily. That's what he needed, the camaraderie, the closeness that surviving together gives a group. Most of his close comrades had been transferred to other places; some were dead. He recalled the trucks full of shouting compas headed for Managua, and himself as part of the small garrison left behind. He would put in for a transfer to Managua—that would fix him. And after that, on to El Salvador. This was going to be a tough road; he'd known it for a long time; he was in for the duration, no matter how hard, long, or lonely. Only pretended to go for Venancia, he told himself, knowing he was going to miss her green eyes. She'd go to Rivas; he'd get a transfer to Managua. It would all work out; this was the beginning of a new era, of a new time. The dead also have a stake in this, he thought, they're going to live a long time in the memory of the living, until we ourselves are forgotten.

He rose half asleep from the cot and fumbled in the dark for the plastic Baggie with the cigarettes. He pulled one out and lit it in his cupped hands, dragging deeply on the tobacco and exhaling a plume of grey smoke. He opened the torn screen door and stared out through the soft curtain of rain toward the darkened garden. It was almost daylight. He was a little older than yesterday; a new dawn would soon crash over the hills. Miriam came briefly into his thoughts; the image in the photo washed away by the interminable rains, the memories like wilted flowers in a vase. Then he thought of his own land, Califas, so very far away, of all that had happened to him there and how he'd come to fight here, so far from where he was born, yet so close.

He stood in the doorway while he finished the cigarette, hearing the last of the wind-whipped rain on the corrugated roof. He imagined all the ethereal dead waiting for him in the wet garden or buried in the hills and cemeteries from East Los to Peñas Blancas, and he pictured all the dead he'd known in his life, and he himself fading away like a mural at Palenque. One day, who knows when, will there be compas to give the last salute to the universe? He felt constantly transforming, like the galaxies in eternal revolutions, like the windswept rain on the roofs of Peñas Blancas watering the vines and plants in the unkept garden. The same rain that once washed down the asphalt streets, palm trees, and con safos-sprayed walls of his barrio was now falling softly over the hand-nailed crosses in the cemetery behind the warehouse, dripping down the barrels of the silent cannons, and gathering in puddles before the barracks where Venancia slept, separated from him by more than the 2-lane highway. He thought of the rain over Nicaragua, of how tomorrow it would sprout green grass and wild flowers on the crater-scarred hills and fill the empty trenches in El Ostional and along the Río Ostallo and Hill 50 with rich, new earth. His mind raced on as he saw the grey cumulus storm clouds rushing swiftly across the sky and first light breaking over a distant hilltop, casting a rainbow over Peñas Blancas. He imagined dawn over the adoquín-strewn streets of Managua, sunrise in the fields of Nueva Guinea and over the great forest of the Segovias and throughout Central America, and he knew the sun would shine today upon all the living and the dead who never die.

Peñas Blancas-San Francisco
"La Misión"
1979-86